FRAMES

ANNA CATMAN

Order this book online at www.trafford.com
or email orders@trafford.com

Most Trafford titles are also available at major online book retailers.

Print information available on the last page.

ISBN: 978-1-4907-8963-7 (sc)
         978-1-4907-8964-4 (e)

Library of Congress Control Number: 2018955544

Our mission is to efficiently provide the world's finest, most comprehensive book publishing
service, enabling every author to experience success. To find out how to publish your book,
your way, and have it available worldwide, visit us online at www.trafford.com

Trafford rev. 08/27/2018

 www.trafford.com

North America & international
toll-free: 1 888 232 4444 (USA & Canada)
fax: 812 355 4082

FRAMES

...for he was a real demon. One day, when he was in a merry mood, he made a looking glass which had the power of making everything good or beautiful that was reflected in it almost shrink to nothing, while everything that was worthless and bad looked increased in size and worse than ever...They carried the glass about everywhere, till at last there was not a land nor a people who had not been looked at through this distorted mirror. They wanted even to fly with it up to heaven to see the angels, but the higher they flew the more slippery the glass became, and they could scarcely hold it, till at last it slipped from their hands, fell to the earth, and was broken into millions of pieces. (Hans Christian Andersen).

What I hate most of all are frames, Nilly told himself, starring into a window. Yes, upcv frames like these. The weather outside was changing all the time, every minute. Rain followed by sun and vice versa.

Once, rather a long time ago now, whenever he paid any attention to weather, which was, basically, all the time, he immediately felt nostalgic. 'How wonderful to live in a flat where you actually feel weather. Or rather see it, differently, because it is divided from you by a solid wall. The weather is out there, and you are here, in a warm, cosy, securely sheltered place. But not anymore. He did not feel this way anymore. How wonderful to live, basically, almost in the street. Open the door, even a little bit, and you see the weather. Or rather it flies in with the wind. Nilly stared into the window frame. They've just changed them and looking into the window was especially pleasant. But it is wonderful, nothing doing, to live in a block of flats. Especially somewhere in the other hemisphere. And when you open the door, you come to a staircase smoked through and through by the neighbours, and then get into an elevator, that takes you down, towards the exit into the wider world. Or up to your own place. Nilly stared into the window.

Somebody once told him that what people live for in the Empire is houses. Unlike people who smoke in staircases, adjacent to flats, somewhere there far away. They live for many different things, each for their own, and often they don't think much about their habitats, contented with the fact that they have some. But not in the Empire. Here people live for houses, and this is something to remember, and never forget, if you want to function and live. One must know what's what and where and what's the best thing to put money into. It may not be the most natural thing for you, but it's an important one.

Nilly stared into the frame and thought about... what did he think about? The difference between ... what d'you call it? What makes you tick, maybe, there, smoking in staircases, and here. Does he know, however, what makes people tick? But in case he'd never get it himself, which seems likely, somebody told him. Houses. He had to make an effort to learn what's what and where and how much, and what's the best thing, but it's all for the best. Nilly tried to be very sensible and stared into the window frame.

But what if they catch him himself and put into a frame? They say cases like this happen more frequently now. For everybody there is a suitable frame somewhere. To find out which one is suitable, you have to take the cv of this particular person, and fit it into a upcv frame. Of course, one has to orient it properly for this, and find the right angle. The name of the frame, however, yucipv, or, in alternative spellings, yuseepeevee, yusipv, and even ucvp, comes from the name of an Old Slavonic letter, or rather two similarly looking letters, big and little yuses, or juses. The little yus looked a lot like the contemporary capital A, with the only difference being an additional stick facing down in the middle of the horizontal line. The big yus looked like letter Y turned upside down, also with one additional stick, inserted in the middle of the angle facing down, a bisector, and a triangle on top. Both corresponded to some kind of nasal vowel sounds in the Old Slavonic, and both disappeared later. The reason why we know that the sounds were nasal is that they left some traces, like m and n, where they were previously. It just so happened that Nilly knew a bit about it. He wasn't quite sure, however, whether it is known, what the nasal sounds actually sounded like. Is it, by any means, like Cicero, he wondered. C sounded in Latin as either k, or ts, not exactly known, but probably k. Although everybody prefers to say ts, at the moment. Something like this? Something completely different, which hasn't, however, left more traces in what we speak now, than this mysterious either k or ts left in what they speak? Only m and n. Triangular frames that looked a lot like modern letters with additional sticks. Throw a rope loop onto the stick and tie somebody to it. Tie yourself. This is what frames are for, to fit things into them, are they not?

What if they catch me, Nilly thought, again, and put into a frame? They say they nail one's limbs to a stick inside a frame, to immobilise you. Arms and hands go into one slot of this stupid frame, legs and feet into another, although, of course, theoretically speaking, one could have separate frames for arms. legs and a head. If one has particularly fast or slow, or beautiful legs, one can have any kind of head on top of them. Or can one not? A writer can be black, a woman, or even disabled, he thought, again, but not all three together. Like a boss in that old folk joke which affirmed that a boss can be a drunkard, a Jew and not a party member, that is, any two of these, but not all three together. The same kind of mechanism at work, or is it?

They put one's head into one slot and arms and legs into another. According to the quality of hat on your head and the toefl score achieved some time. And other similar things. Amazing, Nilly thought. All these scores and what they get them for, one could say it's the whole generation's experience packed and wrapped into them. Maybe even more, than one generation's, although of course, one or two generations before there were no tests' results you had to have. But at the same time, there is no commonly accepted and frequently used way to speak about them. One can speak, at best, about some kind of Spanish-speaking hotel maids, like Jenifer Lopez in that well-known film. One can say something about it, but not too often and not too much truth. It has to appear sufficiently romantic to be acceptable. The rest of it, obviously, is too much for a lay person and social conscience in general. Not to speak about, then. No wonder they try to shave me like Jennifer all the time, and fit into a frame.

Could it be, Nilly thought, that your right leg is in one frame, and the left one – in quite another. Pianists, for example. They use the right pedal all the time, and the left one only sometimes. Although, of course, this is not it, is it?

A guard, one of those people who were responsible for the right match between the frame and a person, came close to him. Nilly stood, immobile like a statue, pushing hard the corners of his frame with his arms and legs. His trunk and tail wouldn't fit at all. As for the trunk, Nilly put most of it into his mouth, although it made him cough all the time. The tail… What to do with it, Nilly couldn't decide at all, and tried to stand so that the guard wouldn't notice. The guard came closer and touched the frame.

'What it's made of?' he asked.

'The frame?'

'Yes, what's the material called?'

'I don't know,' Nilly said. I think it's cheese, cheese crust. Swiss cheese, or, maybe, gouda, I'm not sure.'

'And where is the cheese?' went on the guard.

Nilly wanted to say that he's lost it, or maybe, somebody ate it, but changed his mind.

'There is a little bit left,' he whispered. 'Would you like a cheese fondue?'

It occurred to him that if he feeds fondue to the guard and he'll find it tasty, he may simply ignore his tail and won't think it's inappropriate. All Nilly had to do was to jump out of the frame, take the newly-acquired fondue set, light the fire, and when it'll be ready, feed the guard the melted cheese in a cup with crusty bread. What can be better? But Nilly couldn't push himself to do it. He was afraid. If he leaves the frame, even for a moment, the guard will immediately see his tail. And then... what will happen then, he didn't want to imagine. It would be better to figure out beforehand what's his position about his tail. Before he left the frame and started doing something. Although, of course, even if he does say that he wants fondue, it does not guarantee, one hundred percent, that he will accept the tail. Turn a blind eye to it.

But, after all, he, Nilly, won't be so much ashamed of... hard to tell what... what do they see it like? Being unable to walk over some deeply entrenched prejudice, perhaps, and do something in his own interests. Not being strong-willed and entrepreneurial enough to protect his own interests. He will protect them, immediately.

'Would you like fondue?' Nilly whispered, again, and coughed a lot. The guard nodded. Or, maybe, this wasn't a nod at all. Thinking that it's best to interpret his gesture as a sign of agreement, Nilly left the frame, poured a bit of white wine into a little ramekin he used for this, lighted the fire and cut the cheese into cubes. When all was ready, he brought a ramekin with cheese to the guard. The guard tried and wrinkled his nose.

'No,' he said. 'It's not to my taste. Guards don't eat this.'

Nilly wanted to say that the guard is not exactly to his taste either, but reserved himself.

'Try a bit more,' he said. 'Maybe, you just didn't have a proper taste?'

But the guard shook his head: discussion closed. No more comments.

'Nilly!' he cried, a moment later. 'You have a tail! The tail! How dare you? It's not allowed.'

'Where?' Nilly said, reluctantly. 'Where? Don't make things up, will you?'

'Here you are,' he thought. 'I almost expected it. You can't bribe them, or rather if you do, what happens is absolutely unpredictable.'

'Where?' he said, again. 'Where do you see the tail? I never offered you any fondue, how dare you take it without my permission? It's a serious offense, and you'll be responsible.'

'I haven't eaten, almost,' the guard mumbled.

'You have or you haven't, I haven't offered it to you. And you will be responsible,' Nilly said, again.

On the day when Nilly's complaint against the guard had to be heard, he found himself far away. On that day Nilly was busy in his other frame, also upcv, but made of something else. What it was made of, Nilly forgot, maybe because he never looked at it closely enough. Was it, perhaps, the upper crust of the same Swiss cheese? Another sort of cheese, maybe a soft one? Is it called rind then? I will have a closer better look some time later, he decided, because he was, after all, interested. The second one of the two Nilly's frames was perpendicular to his first frame, the one he jumped out from, to feed fondue to the guard. In the second frame there was very little space for arms and legs, but considerable space allowed for the head. The space for the head was marked with a metal square, within which was fitted a metal circle, touching its sides. The space for the head was so large, it would make one look almost a Cheshire cat, but not quite, because there were, nevertheless, spaces for arms and legs allowed. They just had to be the right size. To see whether one's head fits into the circle frame well enough, one had to tie the person's hair to it. When Nilly stepped inside that second frame, a specially trained auditor (who was not called a guard, but what was the actual difference between them, not everybody knew) divided his hair into a few locks of approximately equal size, and tied them to the frame. The head had to be positioned in such a way as to make the gap between it and the frame no wider, than a few millimetres. To achieve this, the head had to be big enough. Nilly thought hard day and night about how to make his head bigger. Some said one had to think more, others believed that it's best to read more books. Just another group of people remarked, that both thinking and reading are optional, because one can simply arrange one's hair so that it will look more voluminous and fluffy and make the head to appear larger. A hairdresser would do that. Or one can do it oneself, at home. Besides, even hair amateurishly curled at home on little pieces of paper looks like rings and is easier to tie to the frame.

The frame in which Nilly lived on that day, was intended for speaking. In his particular case, speaking about literature. Although, of course, objects of the same or similar structure existed for other purposes.

That morning Nilly woke up early. He felt all sounds his body makes are a bit out of key. What with? Some kind of imaginary symphony, perhaps. On the other hand, it wasn't totally cocophonic and chaotic, either. Just pleasantly contemporary. This was, at least, what Nilly felt. His head was larger, than his usual size. It was literally stuffed with clever thoughts, and his arms and legs were shorter now. Besides, his head seemed larger, because he washed his hair the day before, and curled it. He then sprayed it with a product, to add volume to his hair. Now he was ready to fit into his second frame.

When speaking of literature and the tea that followed were finished with (what did he say? He'd so much like to remember; something about Dostoevsky's novel called 'Double', he did remember now, vaguely). Anyway, when all this was finished, Nilly decided to rush off to that other place, where his complaint against the guard who ate, but didn't appreciate fondue, was considered. The guard, in his own turn, complained about Nilly: he had a tail, a fluffy long tail, and this was simply not allowed by this frame. The one he jumped out from to feed fondue. Nilly hoped that the guard will shut up and turn a blind eye to his tail, but this hope turned out to be vain. He didn't. Maybe, because he didn't want any fondue, but, after all, there was no guarantee he'd allow this from the beginning, anyway. How clumsy his behaviour was! Or, maybe, not so much? We'll see, Nilly decided and rushed ahead. He had to run quickly, to reach there where his complaint was considered on that day, in time. Trying to run in such a way that people won't see his long very voluminous tail, Nilly hurried ahead. He was far away from the place where he needed to be, and to cut the time, he jumped into a train. He looked at himself into the window glass, and stepped back, scared. He can't come like this to see the committee that considered his complaint. His arms and legs were too short, the head visibly too large, and looked as if there was a crow's nest on it, with so many locks, and pins, and curls. What if they won't recognize him at all? This will be what will happen, he was sure.

Panicked, Nilly moved closer to the window glass, trying to see his identification number, written on his arm, in the window glass reflection. His arms were too short now and it was hardly possible at all. Suddenly Nilly noticed, that his arm is now positioned at an angle to the window, and when it is reflected in it, it seems longer. He stood on his toes, trying to put his legs in the same way and to make them appear longer in the window reflection, and he almost managed to do that.

'But I've found the principal solution!' he thought. Nilly was overjoyed. 'If they are going to take a photo of me, I will simply take a mirror with me, and will make my reflection, or rather my arms and legs, longer, and they will fit the frame nicely. Who'll be able to tell, in a photo, and not a large one with that, what's what?'

It wasn't completely obvious to Nilly, how to implement this idea into practice, that is, what exactly should be reflected, and what shouldn't, and what the angles should be, to perfectly fit the frame. But anyway, what mattered was the solution. He's always had a lot of difficulty with all things that require spacial thinking and imagination. Maybe because of this, now he didn't exactly know, where he is. Or, perhaps, it's simply something all people, who happen to transport themselves from one frame into another, share.

He needed a hairdresser who'd make his head seem sufficiently small, as necessary, and also a mirror, to reflect himself and fit into the frame. And he didn't have nearly enough time.

Trying to get there on time, after all, Nilly jumped off the train and rushed to the hairdresser to make his head seem smaller. Then to buy a mirror. When he finally reached the place, where his complaint was considered, it was late. Awfully. Forty minutes late. The meeting was scheduled for four o'clock, and it was now twenty minutes to five. But nobody seemed to pay any attention.

'Maybe, I should try and apply for two frames,' Nilly thought. 'Yes, apply for two frames. Theoretically speaking, I should have a right to fit into two frames. Apply, and out with it, because otherwise they won't let it just be, anyway. My head seems too large. But what to do with the tail? It's not allowed by any of these frames, anyway.'

He was so scared now, that his thoughts drifted and bumped into each other, like some kind of little icebergs, most of them covered by dark and cold water of his subconscious, if this was subconscious, of course. Probably not. And half of them melting on the way. 'Yes, apply for two frames,' Nilly tried to strengthen himself and shook his strangely tousled hair.

'Please sit down,' the committee's Head interrupted his thoughts, when he spoke to all those people in the room. 'Today's agenda is the complaint Nilly made against his guard R. In the centre of which, the complaint, that is, is the cheese fondue Nilly fed to his guard. Tried to feed.'

'Objection, I ate no fondue,' said the guard.

'Tried by whom and what for?' Nilly said.

'Doesn't matter, doesn't matter,' the Head said. 'Tried or didn't try, the fed or state, or not at all and didn't state it, let's call this case, to be concise, the case of Nilly, his guard R. and fondue. Nilly, you're fired. R. is not going to be, as a consequence, your guard anymore. There conflict between you two, is exhausted, consequently. By the way, what's wrong with your arms?

Nilly put a mirror in such a way that his arm was reflected in it and seemed longer. His identification number was reflected, too, and was readable now, but the other arm wasn't. Where his other arm should have been, he put his tail. It will look like another arm, he thought.

'What's that?' the Head said. 'I can see with a naked eye, that your measurements and parameters, Nilly, do not meet the standards allocated to this frame. But to do it by the book, and to follow the rules properly, we'll take your photo, both en face and sideways, and full figure one, and we will match and compare your silhouette with the measurements required by this frame.

When they were taking his photo, Nilly tried to move his tail from one side to another, and to make both arms appear longer. The Head said that the photo had not enough resolution, both Nilly's arms seemed too blurred, and discarded the photo. After that, he had a closer look, and blew his whistle.

'I have a right to fit into two frames!' Nilly cried. 'Stop that!'

'Two frames?' the Head said. 'How did you get the permission?'

'The permission is given to everybody who... who... Nilly stumbled. You know, as well as I do, that the permission is given to everyone who can acquire the measurements, required by a certain frame, during one night. And then, during, let's say, another day acquire the measurements required by another frame.'

'How do you achieve this, Nilly?' the Head asked. 'Your head is again too large, your hair too fluffy and spiky in some places, and your arms and legs too short.'

'It's because they've stolen my hair curlers,' Nilly said.

'What do you mean, because?' the Head said. 'Quite the opposite, in fact, your head would seem smaller. But doesn't matter, doesn't matter, ' he said. 'But what about the tail? Do you have a permission to possess the tail, as well, maybe?'

'God, what to do,' Nilly thought, feverishly. 'Theoretically speaking, there are a few possibilities. It would be wonderful, of course, just to strangle him with the tail, he'd die of asphyxia and this is it. But to reach him... maybe hard... or maybe I can... just stretch harder and reach. Otherwise, I can put the frame on fire. It's made of Swiss cheese, and, of course, it would just melt and collapse, and hopefully, be just the right size after it. My arms and legs will fit into it and won't seem too short anymore. I can shave off all the hair, the head will be smooth and will seem smaller. Also a solution. I can use a mirror, somehow. If you find the right shape and will reflect your body parts there, somehow, and find the right angle, you can seem almost anything you like.

He remembered, vaguely, that he read somewhere, recently, that a mirror which is cylindrical – in old times there were mirrors of all possible shapes – is called an anamorph. Find a mirror like this, or some other, and use it to fit properly into the frame. Although, of course, you have to pass it all for yourself, to get away with it. But in a photo this shouldn't be a problem, either.

'Whether or not you have a right to fit two frames, Nilly,' the Head interrupted his reflections, again, is, arguably, a complicated question. Maybe yes or maybe no. But in any case, you have no right for the tail. And, according to the law of our Empire, we are going to cut it off, bit by bit, with an axe.'

Nilly got up and tried to run away, but a few guards caught him near the exit.

'Now we are going to test, live, whether or not you fit into both your frames, and how well,' the Head told him. 'The tail aside.'

'Clumsy,' Nilly thought. 'Awfully clumsy and stupid. I shouldn't have tried to pass the tail for an arm. What it did was simply attract attention. And everybody told me, that it's clumsy.'

But they've pushed him, already, into the first frame, the one that required long arms and legs. The second one, with a specially designed place for a large head, was placed at the ninety degrees angle to the first one.

'Then they'll turn me sideways and fit into another,' Nilly thought. 'I wonder, which one will they start with?'

The Head made a little sign, and two officials pushed Nilly towards a frame, the first one. At the same time, they kept asking him questions.

'You dropped the medicine, Nilly, that you had to administer to another person,' said one of the officials, solemnly. 'Dropped it on the floor.'

'It's because I was very hurried,' Nilly said. 'I was late on that day, you see. But generally, in normal life, I'm a very punctual person.' Nilly must have felt that it doesn't sound convincing enough. 'At another time of the day,' he added.

'Another time of the day? What time?'

'Any time,' Nilly said. 'The thing is, I had to come where this frame was applied to me, very early. Seven o'clock in the morning, or six. I overslept, simply, once. And it all happened four times a week.'

'Why four?' the Head asked.

'Because on the fifth day, I think, it was Tuesday, I did something different. I functioned in another frame, that is.'

'What did you do?'

'I attended seminars and sometimes even delivered presentations of my own.'

'What about?'

'The Russian language,' Nilly explained, shyly. 'But the Russian language is not much in demand, you see. Russia is far away, and the citizens of our Empire are, simply, not curious enough. Besides, the Empire language is widely-known and in use everywhere. So to learn something else, you really have to want it a lot, and be rather capable,' Nilly said.

'I see,' the Head said. 'Some things are clear to me now. You were very much in a hurry, and this is why you dropped it. But why did you have to be in a hurry? You couldn't come later, could you?'

'I don't know,' Nilly said, honestly. 'Probably not, later was no good for some reason.'

'So what about were your presentations?' the Head said.

'About the Russian language,' Nilly explained again.

'So you're a communist?' the Head asked. 'Reinforce the surveillance,' he added. Nilly threw a furtive glance at his tail.

'A communist?' he asked. 'Why? Oh, Russia.' He understood, at last. 'Yes, probably, I am. A communist. Or a socialist. What's the difference, by the way.'

Whether or not the Head knew, what's the difference, he ignored this last remark.

'A red,' he said. 'Well, well. We'll consider your application for two frames, Nilly, in the due time.'

In the meantime, Nilly thought about what intelligence is. It is, after all, an important concept for fitting frames, or is it not? In other parts of the world, he thought, intelligence is something very different. It's hard to tell precisely, what it is, and how much I may have, but it's clearly something very different. Not at all what it is here. Here, inside the Empire, the Head is very intelligent, for example. And that person, who made me come at seven o'clock in the morning four times a week. He is intelligent too, in his own way. He realized at once, that it's not going to be easy for me, and won. He must be intelligent, then. No, one has to admit, that intelligence is something very different here. But maybe, it's not at all what matters? Some people say, that your physical size, for example, may matter as much. Taller and heavier people are more willingly fitted by their peers into all kinds of frames, even the ones with a head and, of course, all those with long arms and legs. But anyway.

Intelligence must be, Nilly vaguely remembered, an ability to solve problems. But after all, it does matter what problems you want to solve, does it not?

Or take emotional intelligence, he went on. Some people believe, and he knew people like this even among those, who lived, most of the time, within the frame with a large space for a head, that emotional intelligence is most important, when it comes to well-being of your dependants, of any age, especially young ones. And, on the contrary, too much knowledge, of anything, is absolutely unnecessary. It could be hard to convince them, Nilly knew it, that when it comes to reading and understanding the list of ingredients on bottled baby food, additional knowledge can do no harm. Especially, because sometimes there is something not quite right with these ingredients. But no, even people with a large head in a frame, did not believe in knowledge being power in this case. On the other hand, what problems they would solve admitting it? If any. Isn't it just safer, then, to talk of emotional intelligence instead?

After that, Nilly started counting his money. If he does not appear in this first frame of his four times a week, and he won't now, he'll have less of it, obviously. He'll have to stop paying for some things. There will be, what d'you call it? Interest accruing, or does it, perhaps, mean something else? He thought that it may be just the right time to find out what it means, or, perhaps, it would have been better to do it before? But better late, than never and so on. But nobody would let him borrow, if he didn't have to appear in that first frame of his four times a week. This was something he did know, mostly because he's been through it, already. This must be intelligence, too, he thought, in that other sense. Or is it not. Maybe, they meant it from the start? Or did they not?

'What's the normal procedure for considering an application for two frames?' he asked. 'And how much time is it going to take?'

'To consider your application, Nilly, we have to take a few steps,' the Head said. 'We'll take a photo of you, both en face and sideways, and at a few different angles, and compare the photos with the parameters of the two frames. Besides, each photo will be compared to you personally. But this is to happen later, after the comparison of photos with frames has been completed. The most complicating thing is your tail. If it wasn't for the tail, all this should take no longer, than a few days.'

The Head stumbled, for a few moments, and gave Nilly a little brochure.

'Here,' he said. 'Everything is explained in clear plain English. Your right for two frames and everything else.'

Nilly read the brochure, and then asked a question.

'Tell me,' he said, 'why do you prefer structures, I mean, frames, which are so inflexible? Rigid, even? All your frames could look completely different. It's just a bit like a little tree, of which each branch has a slot for some kind of info, like a place where a fruit can grow. For example, if it's a restaurant frame, it has slots for location, price, number of stars, which is not the quite the same as price, though similar, number of seats and so on. Why aren't your youseepeevees similar?'

'But they're similar,' the Head said.

'No,' Nilly said. 'No, they are not. They are all so inflexible. And why should I fit into them at all? Who thought it up?'

'And also,' the Head said, 'the law is the law. That's the way these frames are created. No slots are provided.'

'Alright,' Nilly said. 'Then do this. Why not unite, amalgamate, or blend, whatever, two frames into one. Three, even. Then I wouldn't need any permission for two frames.'

'How?'

'Elementary.' Just put a slot, pardon me, the place allowed for a head in the second frame into the first one, with longer arms and legs. Push one frame inside another, and maybe, average the length of legs. And see, what happens. By the way, it's quite possible to find something, that fits both frames well enough.'

'What's that?' the Head said.

'Well, in my case, it is, probably...' Nilly stopped. He felt shy. 'It's something like sign language, I think. It requires a head, but can't be done without hands, obviously. Really, how can you sign with no hands?'

Nilly was so excited about this idea to unite, amalgamate, or blend, whatever, two frames into one, that he started looking for a place, where he could learn the sign language. But it turned out not to be easy, if not to say impossible. A few possibilities he's found turned out to be simply fakes – dates announced were incorrect and advertised locations non-existent. If there were some possibilities left, most of them would require more time and money, than Nilly was prepared to put into it. Especially, at first, as a first attempt. Later, maybe, he'd put into it more, if he was allowed to make a not very heavy-weight-lifting first attempt. But there was nothing like this, it seems. Really, he thought, our Empire treats many different things in the same way. The less you know about them, the better, apparently.

'Now we'll take pictures of you, Nilly,' the Head said. 'And then compare them with the two frames, for which you wish to acquire a permit, and also compare with you.'

Nilly was unhappy about his photos.

'I'm much taller, in real life,' he said. 'Really, have a look for yourself. Look in the mirror.'

'It's not about what you see, when you look in the mirror, Nilly,' the Head said. 'Any picture is a document. The process of comparison of a person and his photo is a process of establishing factual correspondences.'

'Factual correspondences?' Nilly said. 'But this photo has nothing to do with reality.'

'Which reality?' the Head said. 'What is it?'

'The real reality. The true one. There is such a thing as objective reality out there, and we feel it. We know it by all our senses. Or we know it, because it produces certain sensations, like visual and auditory. We hear, see and smell it. Who's said that?'

'Think for yourself, Nilly,' the Head said. 'What's the difference between you and your picture? Your picture looks exactly like you. At a distance, just a few steps away, there is no difference at all. And especially no difference, if you take a photo of each, and put it into a frame.'

'A photo of each which?' Nilly said.

'Well, of course, a photo of you in the frame, and a photo of your reflection, in a mirror, in the same frame,' the Head said, patiently. 'What's the difference? To your senses? But are they the same thing?'

'It's not the same thing, anyway, even if it looks the same,' Nilly said. 'Think for yourself. If there is a mirror in a frame, and I see a reflection there, say, of a tree, it means that the tree is somewhere very close. It's close enough to be reflected. But if there is a photo of a tree in the frame, it doesn't mean this. It means, me or somebody else has seen a tree, taken a photo and put inside the frame.'

'Reality is given to us by our five senses. Sensations is what we know it by,' the Head said. 'And what do your senses tell you here?'

'They don't tell me anything, I know,' Nilly said, stubbornly.

Suddenly he thought about what everybody knew: each frame, to be used for life, or even for a while, came with a trial period. Shorter or longer, but there had to be one. For some frames, however, it was significantly shorter, than for other, for whatever reason. For example, in his first frame, the one with long arms and legs, it was just a couple of months. Unlike that for the second frame, with the large head slot: it was usually no less than a year. Strange, Nilly thought. If I actually had a couple of months to get used to it, it seems quite likely that I'd stop oversleeping and making mistakes that come from being in too much hurry. But, somehow, I didn't have that long to get used to it. Perhaps this person, with his intelligence-in-quite-another-sense, thought something like this: in a couple of months, only a very lazy or a very stupid person won't get used to it. So, if I need to act, I need to act quickly. Otherwise, it may be too late to get rid of this person. Nilly was close to congratulating himself on having understood what intelligence in this-quite-another-sense means. At last. Strange, he thought again. When you come to think of it, in that other frame, the second one, the one with the large head, the trial period is longer. But also long enough for everybody, except very lazy and very stupid, to learn. But again, I've never had a chance to use all this time. The same kind of logic, perhaps, Apparently, this intelligence-in-quite-another-sense worked quite similarly in both cases.

'What do you know, Nilly?' the Head said. 'And how? Look at both pictures and you'll see, that you are who you are, yourself, that is.'

Nilly's picture wasn't very clear and was too much blurred, but smiled and spoke the language of the Empire. It was repeating all the time the same sentence. To be used with conviction, if you want to fit into a frame, and absolutely untranslatable. Nilly just realized, that it is absolutely untranslatable. Like a lot of that stuff that had something to do with frames, but anyway. 'I'm passionate about helping people achieve their full potential,' Nilly's head was repeating. At some point in time, Nilly was ashamed to use this phrase to fit into a frame. But then, later, he got used to it. Strange, he thought again, I heard, at least, once, this phrase to be used in its proper and literal sense. To be more precise, I read it. It was part of a reference letter somebody has written for me, to help me fit into another frame. But shortly after all this place, where they used phrases like this in the proper and literal sense, stopped to exist. Nilly wondered for a while, whether the phrase was too real, to be used to fit into phantom things like phrames. Or was it, perhaps, that not many thought it means a good thing, although it was mandatory for some situations, like fitting yourself into a frame.

The Head stood close to him and kept insisting, that Nilly looks a lot like his picture. 'I wonder,' Nilly thought, 'does he have a trial period? And if so, how long is it? And why on Earth, kings, tsars and presidents don't have it? Quite the opposite. Only the lazy and indifferent don't talk about a couple of years not being long enough for establishing some kind of ambitious policy, or whatever it's called. Achieve something, and so on. School children, students and just people who need good quality care can't be offered second-rate product for more, than a few weeks. But, apparently, it does not apply to just people who live somewhere, be it a city or the Empire. Because a couple of years is said to be not long enough.'

Nilly looked at his photo. A few minutes later the Head announced to Nilly his decision.

'We allow you two frames, Nilly,' he said, solemnly. 'Here's your written permission. In your particular case, they will be at an angle to each other, and will have a common axis. Rotating around it, they will look a bit like a turnstile, or a turntable.'

'A lazy susan?' Nilly asked.

'No, not quite. It's more like a rotator door than a plate,'

'I see,' Nilly said.

'As you enter, you will be able to go through one frame, and as you exit, you can jump into another, why not.'

'As I enter where?' Nilly asked. 'And what about the measurements? To meet the requirements of these two frames, I need to have two different sets of parameters.'

'As you enter where each frame will take you,' the Head said. 'It's your responsibility to see, where it will take you. As for parameters, while you are, where each frame takes you, you can change your parameters, according to the requirements of the next frame. Tying hair to a phrame is not part of fitting frames procedure anymore,' the Head concluded.

''Not bad,' Nilly thought. 'Could be worse.'

He discovered, recently, that if you just scratch a frame hard enough, it can result in you finding yourself in a completely new place. Parameters mean something different there, and the corresponding frames, too. Some are not even based on measuring, but on something else.

With time, Nilly developed a habit of carrying a lot of broken mirror pieces in his pockets. Especially, if he had to go out. They could always come handy, if somebody stopped him and tried to see, how well he fits into both his frames. At least, he could make his visible parameters meet the requirements of the frame, using the broken mirror pieces in his pockets. Somewhere there in the looking glass the two images would meet and satisfy some auditor's demanding eye. Talk of reality given to us by our senses.

By the way, Nilly thought, some languages have more, than one word for reality. Russian, for example. But English doesn't seem to have too many alternatives. Realm? What's the difference between reality and realm? Can you always substitute one for another? It seems you can.

Reality, given to us by our senses. How many, by the way? Blind people, say, don't see at all. Does it mean they have another reality? Because what their senses give to them is different?

'Reality, given to us by our senses,' he said, loudly. 'I can give you reality,' he told the Head. 'Or realm. By the way, what's about the tail?'

'Given to you, not to us,' the Head said. 'to you.'

'To us,' Nilly said. 'Because it's what's common knowledge.'

'What?'

'Reality.' Nilly breathed in a lot of air and breathed it out into the Head's ear.

'Us doesn't have to include me,' the Head said. 'There are different kinds of us. There is an inclusive us, and exclusive one, that does not include the person who you're speaking to. Which us do you mean?'

'What do you think?' Nilly said. 'Reality is what we all know. Right? By the way, what is senses? Our five senses?'

'What are senses?' the Head said, like an echo.

'Senses provide us with sensual experience,' Nilly said. 'It's how we know, what reality is. For example, if I start tickling you with my tail, it's going to be given to us by your senses. Or given to you?'

Needless to say, Nilly has acquired a right for his tail, as well. But before it happened, he often had to find new and new pieces of broken mirror, when he ran out of them. One day, unexpectedly, a piece got into the committee's Head eye.

AESOP AND BEADS

Nilly was constantly preoccupied with the question of hiding his doubtful, he was sure of it, in a normal law-abiding person's eyes, writing. When he was not preoccupied with this, he was busy with some contingent, so to speak, questions. Such as what exactly makes it doubtful. What's a law-abiding person and what rules they live by. Are they law? Probably not, but then what are they? We all have an image, but what's in it? If there is something solid inside it, what is it? Otherwise, where does it come from and how it was created?

But anyway, whatever was at work here, what to do? Maybe use another language, his first one? It's so much more natural, besides, a law-abiding person's expectations can be different. But everybody, it seems, can read just about anything these days. Who knows, how it happens. Pure energy of thought? Automatic translation? Something else, altogether unknown to him? But whatever it was, it seems to be true. Maybe, use a secret code? Something like code break puzzles use? As this was, basically, all Nilly knew about codes and decoding, he abandoned this idea. The problem is, he thought, all these scribblings somehow break some kind of code. That's the problem. But how to deal with it? Even scribbling it in just one more language, breaks the code a bit more, if this is possible. It can hardly be a solution then. Although, of course, who said that one shouldn't break codes? Or push boundaries. The latter, certainly, seems to be encouraged, by all kinds of encouragers of literary pursuits. Is breaking codes the same thing as pushing boundaries, with a p, Nilly wondered. And if not, what's the difference.

Of course, the most acceptable behaviour could be not to write things down at all. Not to leave any evidence behind, any traces. One can simply learn by heart everything you want to remember. People did do this. But this method can be used, most successfully, with poetry. And poetry was not something he could think of recently.

Another possible way, he thought, would be to write things down on a sheet of paper and swallow it. But it's going to be digested, if, of course, your digestion is OK. What else is there left?

He remembered, suddenly, that clams, for example, - or what are they? Some kind of molluscs, anyway – do not digest, instantly, everything that gets inside them, with food. Some really hard particles – real pieces of hard matter – do not dissolve at all. They stay forever inside them. And little by little they become covered by layers of that beautiful translucent mother- of-pearl substance. And in the end become pearls. He remembered how he's seen, as a child, a wonderful exhibition with his grandparents. Some kind of virtuoso artisan – was he oriental? Probably not? It was impossible to recall this now – used microscopically small objects as background for his art. He painted pictures on rice grains, wrote poetry and manifestos on pearls, and covered wooden matches with incredibly complicated marquetry and other designs. A lot of it was made of precious and semi-precious stones, all very small, and to see the result, one had to use special equipment, strong lenses and microscopes.

But what a wonderful idea. Can one write a whole novel like this, on pearls? Nilly wondered. But why not? If somebody could write important messages on them. Write a chapter on each of the pearls you have and also an author's portrait and a short annotation on the book's content and his or her biography. The latter should be placed on the largest pearl and can be suspended on a chain from the rest of the necklace, as a pendant. Pendant, Nilly sighed. Why should one want to call something like this with a word like that? But they do. And after that, one can give somebody this beautiful object as a present, for birthday and other occasions.

Among other kinds of Aesopian machinations, aimed at hiding or coding the content, this seems as a sufficiently good one, Nilly thought. What will I need?

What I lack, Nilly thought, gloomily, is skill. Or manual dexterity, as they call it. To make something like this, you need tools. They cut all these pearls with something, after all. Or burn them. He wasn't sure what the process is called, but there certainly was something complicated involved. You need lenses, Nilly thought, a strong one, with that, or maybe even a microscope, depending on the size. By the way, he remembered, one can buy a microscope, and cheaply.

Thinking about where to buy what you would need to realize this idea, technically complicated and witty as it was, Nilly started browsing through printed notices on the wall of a building he stood next to. God, why should I be so clumsy, he thought. From all the endless spectre of human competence, there is only one thing available to him: speak. And, perhaps, speak about speaking, meta-speak, that is. Whether or not he can do this well enough is another question, but he certainly can't do anything else. Nilly sighed. When it comes to something else, he's helpless like ... like... like who knows who...

Thinking like this, Nilly stumbled upon an interesting notice. 'Speak on pearls,' it said. 'Printing and editing upon request within 48 hours.' Or was it squeak, rather than speak? Squeak on pearls. Nilly wasn't sure and scrutinised the notice really hard, holding it closely to his eyes. The letter that was following s looked like something in between p and q. Nilly couldn't decide, whether it's facing right or left. The tail was sticking out to the right, he thought, and the semi-circle to the left. Q, then. Squeak on pearls. Not to be confused with speaking, done in oral, obviously, and writing, done on paper and computer. And typing machines, previously. What kind of processes and chemicals they would use to squeak on pearls, Nilly didn't exactly know. Did it matter? It can, under some circumstances.

Nilly calculated, immediately, that if he'd give up drinking coffees on bus stops for a while, as well as chicken pies, then, probably, he won't need much time to save for squeaking on pearls. Just a couple of weeks will be enough, he thought, or, maybe, three. This was his estimate. Maybe even he'll have enough money for his portrait. On a pearl. How wonderful it should be to attach to a novel, squeaked on a pearl, one's portrait. By the way, do they use natural pearls? Can one take artificial ones? What are they called, plastic? Are they cheaper? More expensive? How much time will it all take? How long will it be readable? What if you take plastic pearls – the mother-of-pearl-like covering on them can be destroyed very quickly, he knew it from experience, if one just put on gloves in winter. But what about cultured fresh-water pearls? Are they the same, as natural, in terms of their physical qualities? Or not? Cultured is a bad word. There is life, which includes, they think, houses, probably, and jobs, and there is culture. What's another word for cultured pearls? Grown? What if they squeak my novel on grown cultured fresh-water pearls? Won't that be wonderful? What about black pearls? Pink ones? Possibilities seemed endless to Nilly. And use the largest most beautiful pearl for my portrait, he thought, dreamily. Let it hang in the middle of the necklace, on the chest. Was it called a pendant? Somehow they always had bad words for the best things, he thought, and spoil everything. Maybe I can even print one of my best photos on a pearl, Nilly thought.

He decided not to ask, for now, whether or not it was possible. And if it is, how are they going to transfer his portrait on a pearl. It's best to place my order now, he thought. Not to shoo away the luck. Not that this approach always worked, in fact, he didn't remember it work moderately often, but it seemed the best one in the current situation. I can always ask about my photo on a pearl later, Nilly thought.

When the time came and Nilly received his order, he was shocked. They squeaked it quickly, this was true, but how strangely it all looked! A few chapters of his novel swapped places with each other, the first one was now the second from the end, but the last one, on the other hand, was placed closer to the start of his narrative. Besides, a few chapters were missing altogether. As for the portrait... However hard Nilly tried, he couldn't see himself in this portrait. It looked most similar, he thought, to Edith Piaf. Suddenly he remembered how he bought, recently, two different paperbacks by a well-known detective authoress. And found two different portraits of that same authoress on the last pages of them. There were two, according to the number of bought books. Two different women looked at him from above the books' short annotations. One was a blonde, another one a brunette, with curly hair. Nilly wanted so much, suddenly, to find what the authoress really looked like, that he searched the web. And found some kind of 'averaged' image: the woman's eyes were like the brunette's, the hair like the blonde's, but darker. The mouth was somewhere half-way in- between, and the nose too. A blended, right-in-the-middle of everything image. It seemed supernatural. And now, the same thing. Supernatural.

Thinking that what he saw on that pearl can, by no means, be him, or can it? – Nilly asked the woman at the counter a question.

'Tell me,' he said, 'where is my photo? This is not me, I'm sure.'

'Sure?' the woman said. 'And why do you think so?'

'But see for yourself,' Nilly pressed on. 'Look and see.'

'What do you want me to see?' the woman said. 'And how?'

'How? Through a microscope, of course. The way you've made it, now look and see.'

'You must be kidding me,' the woman said. 'The squeaking specialist is the only one here who has a microscope. We don't use them at the counter. They are only for drawing images.'

'How can you tell one person's image from another, then?' Nilly asked.

'No way. We can't.' the woman said.

Nilly was stunned and overwhelmed and stepped aside to think. If his portrait was somewhere, deep inside these premises, where they took squeaking orders and completed them, how can he find it? How to capture it? And finally, transport it where he wants it to be?

These were all very complicated questions, and he didn't know what to start with.

Let's say, he'll get inside. He'll have to bring a microscope there, to tell one pearl image from another. And then, quietly, get outside with the right pearl and a microscope. How?

If just the pearls were larger, he wouldn't need a microscope to look at them, then. It would be wonderful, Nilly thought, to have something like that magic mushroom Alice in wonderland ate. If you bite on one side of it, you grow taller, bite on another, grow smaller. Or was it something else, not a mushroom, to grow smaller? Anyway. He needs a magic mushroom. But for pearls.

Somebody must have felt his need, because soon Nilly stumbled upon another ad. In the local paper. It offered to buy, for a moderately high price, a certain kind of substance, in a tube, that made everything it was smeared on, larger. Tens and dozens times larger. You wouldn't even have to smear it, probably, because it came with a nozzle and could be sprayed on things. It was a bit like that shrink they used on plastic bags, but working in the opposite direction.

When, using the dark as his cover, during the night-time absence of the counter woman, Nilly sneaked inside the squeaking-on-pearls premises, where he hoped to find his portrait and missing chapters, there were pearls everywhere, and more pearls, aligned in rows and squares on special little trays. But he couldn't find what he was looking for. It was easy, however, to spray all these pearls with a magic substance he brought with himself. When there was just very little left, and it wouldn't spray anymore, he spread it with his fingers. He had just enough for what he found on the trays there. The pearls started growing and were now as big as ostrich eggs. Some even larger, than this. It was easy to read what was written on them. But, alas, Nilly could find only one of his lost chapters there. The rest of it, that he regretted just as much, wasn't there. There was no portrait of him, either, although he found somebody who looked, in fact, very similar. When he finished, he had to decide, how to bring that one enlarged pearl with him. He hasn't thought about it. Pushing it before him, Nilly was striding towards the exit.

But what to do with the rest of it? To buy another tube like this, Nilly thought, and come again? Maybe later. But wouldn't it be easier, after all, to get inside with a microscope, and, instead of smearing the pearls with a magic substance, to look at them all?

And this is what he did, a few days later. It was dark, and he almost smashed that costly piece of equipment, the microscope, against the door frame. Somehow it brought to mind the old Russian phrase, nail the nails with a microscope. But having salvaged the microscope, Nilly found what he was looking for.

VOODOO

What it's most similar to, is voodoo, Nilly was saying, stumping his feet with force and staring into the dark. He was waiting for a bus. Why voodoo, and what it was, really, who knows. But somebody once told him, or, maybe, he read somewhere, or, perhaps, it was just a common belief, hard to tell now, anyway, he knew, that voodoo is, basically, the name of a rather frightening picture: a doll with cut-out eyes which means harm inflicted to some far-away enemy, or a rival. Somebody said once that this was voodoo. All people believed, once, that this was voodoo, although voodoo was, if you tried to find something about it, something African mixed with something Christian, or Catholic. But this was all a normal person would remember about voodoo, Nilly was sure. This kind of strangely magical idea of human impact. If done with proper skill, reaching its aim, unfalteringly. When and where in voodooist spaces – does it matter? – everywhere, presumably.

Nilly tried hard to see something, but couldn't see anything. Looking into the dense darkness now – the electric display that showed when the next bus would be coming and at the same time shed a bit of light on everything was taken away, for whatever reason, - looking into the darkness Nilly was waiting for the bus with a certain number. A happy number. The number coincided with that year, the last one, when everything was ok. 2012. It should be coming now. Nilly will jump inside, touch the reading machine with a special card, the magnetic strip on it, or whatever it was. He'll touch the machine with his card and it will make the right sound. Squuee. Or, with some other machines, foo. Foo, and then, when you take the card away from the machine, ss. Foo-ss. Or did they mean fuss, really? Ready. Just do it all again, when you get off, and, if you want to, in the middle, if you want more foo-ss. Food? Fuss? Just don't forget to top it up.

To top it up economically, Nilly usually bought a weekly pass for his zone, not the central one. If he had to go to the central one, it was enough just to add a little bit more on top of that pass. Or otherwise if he couldn't afford it, he could always just follow somebody very closely getting through that gate where he had to use the card, to open the door and get inside the train. Simply walk in somebody's steps, literally. Also a solution, and not a bad one in its ingenuity. The magnetic card was called a keycard, myki, my key. Who had a wonderful idea that this kind of imagery, as it's called, should be applied to buses and trains? Somebody did, obviously. Perhaps there really was a connection, just he wasn't always happy to see it.

Sometimes Nilly felt really itchy to go somewhere very far, on a train, not really a subway inside the Empire, because it was not riding underground, but that's the best thing, one could always look into the window at one's surroundings. This was a real bliss, Nilly thought. He realized he's always thought this is the very essence of real innocent bliss, even without thinking about it. Nilly wanted it to be innocent bliss, but somebody who's thought up the imagery, perhaps, wanted it to be erotic? Kind of? Innocent bliss is the most costly thing, Nilly thought, unexpectedly. Is it the reason why it's so much disliked around me?

Riding on trains was a real bliss, although it could cost a few additional dollars. He tried to avoid leaving his magnetic card in debt, however. When it was in minus, unpleasant things would happen. This was superstitious, of course, but here you are, these things are bound to mean something, as long as they are used by everybody, are they not? If there was a money sum he thought not unhappy one, at least, on the card, everything was so much better and went smoothly. If there was, at least, two fifty on the card, or three dollars, everything went so much better, he thought, again. On the other hand, if there was too much money, or too little, all went wrong. He really hated to leave the card in munus.

I wonder, which part of me can be squeaking there, Nilly thought, starting to eye the reading cards machine at the bus door and rehearsing the movements he has to do, to reach it in one step and quickly enough; otherwise he could fall, he knew, although his balancing ability was perfectly alright. Peeeping, oinking and squawking, asking for food, kissing and so on. When the card was in minus, however, all went not so well.

Now Nilly was staring into the dark, waiting for the bus with a certain number. There were just a few minutes left, but when it was the time and the bus was there, it was not the number he was waiting for. It happened, sometimes. Somewhere there where they sipped coffee and smoked cigarettes, and bought hot takeaways, and, perhaps, could swap places, let one bus come before another, that had to come first. For whatever reason it happened especially often when Nilly was waiting for a bus with a certain number. Apparently, somebody somewhere there knew what he was waiting for, and didn't want to meet his expectations. It would be better not to let them know that I'm here and what I'm waiting for, Nilly thought. But how to do it? And especially, with a magnetic card? Of course, he could simply not to touch on, but then all this wouldn't count, or would it? What's the use of waiting for a bus with a certain number then, if you don't use your myki card? Thinking about whether or not it will count, if he doesn't use his card, Nilly decided to wait a little more. After all, if you don't touch on, there is always a chance to be caught and get a fine. No, it's better to wait a little bit more.

Nilly decided to have a coffee in a café opposite the bus stop. He could see it well from there. And if the bus he was waiting for will come, he'll have enough time to finish his coffee in one swallow and to reach the bus. Sometimes Nilly would get off from one bus, with a bad number, and start running for another bus, with a suitable good number. The best way to see which one was coming was just look out of the window. If it wasn't too dark outside, this was quite possible. If the speed was rather high, however, it was difficult to do. Because there was some plastic covering on the windows, a kind of net or rather thin membrane, with little holes in it. It came in a few different colours, red, black and yellow, and when, sometimes, Nilly found a torn off piece of it in the street, he thought it was a real treasure, and would pick it up and take home. One can make a bracelet out of it, if, for example, one would put something that helps it to hold its shape inside, like a drinking straw. But stuck on a window, this net made it difficult to see the number of an approaching bus. Maybe, this was what it was here for?

But these days, Nilly thought, the easiest way to see the number of an approaching bus is near the train station. When they lowered the boom gate, everything stops for an enormously long time, and waits until they let go. Because instead of one crossing across the railway tracks there will be two now. One crossing underneath, for the trains, and another one above it, for people. And it's all called removal level crossing. Nilly thought vaguely, probably, for the first time now, that the word level in this phrase must be a hint. What are they getting at? What level? Now there will be two instead of one. Why two and not three. But two is more than one, no doubt about it. But where? It can't be that they want it to be everywhere. Everybody will be sorted into levels, according to... According to what may be not known yet, but perhaps, better not to ask.

Nilly was sipping coffee and thinking about levels, not without pleasure, even. The word level reads the same left to right and right to left. What does it mean? It can't mean, anyway, that they are the same, whatever way you look at it, no matter where you start from. Or can it?

Only drunks and people unable to drive, for whatever reason, ride on trains here. He said it somewhere, recently. Somewhere in a train carriage, when a fellow passenger started a conversation. Drunks, people unable to drive and also, perhaps, all those who ride for work to city, because it's too expensive to park there and better ride a train. But at some other places on Earth, other, better places, it can be different. Nilly sighed. It can be absolutely normal to ride on a bike everywhere. But not here, for whatever reason. What can be the reason, I have no idea, Nilly thought. But it can be awfully hot here. Coffee was finished now, but no bus was in sight.

Nilly decided, that he must find something to eat. It's been a long time, and he felt hungry. He fished a few coins out of his purse and asked for a chicken pie.

At last he saw the blindingly bright bus lights, and, half-covering his eyes with his hand, saw the number. It was the number he was waiting for. At last. Nilly jumped inside. He'll touch on his card on the machine now, it'll squeak and everything is going to be well. And as quick – bite off a piece of a chicken pie. He stretched his hand to find his card in his back pocket.

He's found his card, but it was crossed by a long zigzag crack. Where did it come from? Nilly thought that it might be still usable and this will not stop him, magnetic or whatever they are, qualities should be intact. But they weren't. The touch didn't make any sound it should have, when touched against the machine. Nilly's found another one in his wallet, but it turned out to be in deep minus. If the first one was working, he wouldn't have to pay at all. But it turned out to be broken and didn't. How could it happen? Somebody could, maybe, take it out of his pocket to use. A bit hard to imagine it, because it really has to be someone very poor, but, let's say, maybe. Theoretically speaking, it's possible. Of course, it's hard to find such a person, because one can always get through that automatic gate without any card, if one can't pay at all, But yes, maybe. But then they wouldn't, probably, put it back? Cut it up and put it back in his pocket where it was, it's a bit over the top, is it not? What kind of craziness it should involve, by they way? How obsessed one has to be with the whole symbolic business to do something like this? And some kind of virtuoso skill. To do it so that no one would notice, would require some pick-pocket skill. Pick-pocket is what it was called some time, but is it now? I wonder, if they can, actually, kill for this card, Nilly thought.

What's best, Nilly thought, is the card with a suitable number. A happy one. Once he's found a card with a beautiful number on the ground. Somebody's lost it? Left here, because found another one? Something else? Anyway, Nilly used it for a while, blissfully, and was totally happy. Maybe, more so in his imagination, but anyway. A week, two, three? But then all this cutting up happened. And now what?

All these cards, however, started with 038. 38 was not a good number for Nilly, but somebody thought it's a suitable one to start all these cards with. It was an even one, true, but, on the other hand, why did it remind him so much of eleven? And what did it mean? Maybe, it didn't matter and didn't mean anything at all, because they all started with it. No contrast, then. What matters is what they end with, and what's in the middle. He used the happy card he found until he lost his wallet. Strange, there was almost no money in it. Only cards with numbers many of which he really liked. And regretted having lost them. How could this happen? Nilly didn't know. A really poor person would, probably, take a wallet with some money in it. And choose another place for his actions. What was he going to buy then? Nilly remembered, quite clearly, that what he wanted then was a pair of shoes. They cost four dollars there. And everybody around him were trying on something like that. Strange place to choose for a crime, Nilly thought. Unless, of course, it's a special kind of crime. What do you call it? There is a crime de passion, and this can be called... maybe a crime de symbol? It's when you take, say, a card, or some kind of similar object, useful only to its legitimate possessor, because you don't want the aforesaid possessor to have a card with this number. Who said it can't be? It maybe just a next logical step in the evolution of something...

What do you call it? Crime de symbol, maybe? You have to be fetishist about something, and the rest of it may feel just not interesting enough. Anyway.

Suddenly he remembered a man he met somewhere between two trains, when he was waiting for one. Some kind of really middle-aged, closer to the older side of it, some obscure Middle-Eastern person. Even the look of them, Nilly thought, is reassuring. You may start believing, that not all that's left on this Earth is pure evil. The man spoke very, almost impossibly today, broken English. And helped himself a lot with his hands and face. But there was something he really wanted to tell. The English, he said. The Australian. They are so... he shook his head and made a little gesture near his lips. Like he was pinching two sides of a ravioli together. Tight-lipped, is what he meant. They are - he showed again – no-no – no speak. Tight-lipped. I've been here so many years. But they are...all of them, tight-lipped. Silent. Conformist. And the rest of it in this sense.

Nilly agreed, said something, loudly. Made a sign in the air, to show, what he means. And then the train came. It was time to go.

OSTRICHES

This is how it happens, Nilly thought. To them, ostriches. He felt he's made a discovery. This is how it happens, who could have thought. Was it really the first time he saw it? Was he burying his head in sand all the time before? He wasn't able to tell. Maybe both. But he felt he's found something he didn't know before. This is how it happens that they start throwing chairs in the air.

When C. first asked him to take that girl, M. outside the classroom to work with her, he was a bit taken aback. Why the hell, why should I do it, she is such a pleasant girl, and very calm with that, too, to the point of being almost apathetic. But he didn't say anything. It's better not to quarrel. And especially now, more than ever. He's been with them such a long time. From almost twenty years ago, when he first discovered, there's such an option, to go somewhere and work for free. And then, after a while, can be quite a while, though, you'll be able to ask them for that damn thing. Totally unknown in some other parts of the world, a reference. And this was what he did. Worked for free for a while, volunteered, that is, and then asked for that damn thing, a reference. And then went off to work somewhere not for free, for somebody else.

All this was finished now, for whatever reason. Nilly as usual believed it was the 'system' that was guilty. Before it became so guilty, it was all much easier and made more sense. But whatever the reason, maybe he was simply burying his head in the sand all the way through, now he was back, working for free.

He didn't think, at first, it mattered much. Wherever you go, isn't it all the same? It matters, what you do. And also, possibly, what you think about it all. In this respect, putting your head in some remote and insulated place, be it sand or something else, could be an advantage. But the girl was upset. She wanted to be inside the room, not outside, with all the other people, who sat around the table. Everybody were the other four or five people from the same group of intellectually disable people who came there for classes in what had a somewhat disappointing name of literacy. Literacy was reading and writing, taught by the same new person, C. Some time before there were books, and computers with all kinds of entertaining programs used, and different kinds of books, too. Easier and more difficult ones, to cater for all tastes. All this was gone now, computers were still in the room, but not much in use, and books nowhere in sight. Literacy became writing rather than reading, perhaps, because most of these people were overly clumsy, and hardly able to enjoy writing, unlike reading, which they were able to enjoy, unless stopped.

'I must make no scene,' Nilly told himself. Why he should make no scene and didn't quarrel, he didn't ask himself. Perhaps because he had to get that damn thing, a reference, and go somewhere else not to do this for free. Again. Doesn't it make sense? Actually, he stopped seeing how it made sense, but tried to think so.

The girl was upset. She wanted to be inside, with other people, not outside. They talked and played games, at times, and if you were a good person, obviously, you were allowed to be inside. Everybody went outside, in the hall, and sat at the same table she was sitting at, according to C's order, all the time, during their lunch break. And teatimes. They've always observed teatimes. But she didn't want to eat. She didn't want any tea, either, maybe, because she didn't have any money on her, to buy something from a café as everybody did at times. She wanted to be inside. And she was a good person, wasn't she? Always so calm and slow. You had to tell her to do everything twice. Three times, even. And now this didn't help. It was the second day Nilly spent with her in the hall. To start a day, she had to find the right stamp and stamp today's date on a new page. Nilly vaguely remembered, that at some point in time they all wrote a date. A date was what most of them knew how to write. Copied the date written by a teacher on the blackboard, perhaps. But not anymore. Nilly didn't know, what stamp they had to use, but the girl knew. And how it worked, too.

She kept asking, why she wasn't in. Not finding, what to say, Nilly tried to distract her. 'Look,' he said. 'There's somebody else here, too.'

Somebody else was a non-verbal guy who'd clap his hands at every happy event he could think of, which were many. But he wouldn't say a word. He also tried to be helpful, and when he picked up a hot kettle and wanted to fill the girl's cup with hot water, for tea, Nilly almost allowed it to happen. It was all so close and much at hand in the hall. But Nilly managed to jump and stop the guy just in time. The girl didn't need to be burned with hot water, on top of it. Maybe he didn't have to? He wouldn't burn her, anyway? But only those who knew him really well, could tell, and Nilly wasn't one of them. In fact, there weren't any of them around. Anyway.

What was around were a few printed sheets with some kind of augmented communication table on them. Nobody looked at them, nor asked non-verbal Rob to choose any of the four options, food, water, toilet and something else. Teacher? Rob didn't use that table on a printed sheet, because nobody tried to make him to, in the first place, but it was here close at hand, multiple copies of it lying everywhere. Was it the reason why he was rushing around with a hot kettle? Who knows, and to find out, you have, at least, to eliminate this and that, and the printed sheet.

Drawn out of her rather dream-like state by Nilly who jumped to stop hot water pouring into her cup, the girl seemed only half-awake. She'd certainly be no danger inside. There must've been another reason, then, why they've thrown her out. She was looking for answers and couldn't find any. She stared at the printed sheet, divided into four little squares, for all important things. Is she like that?

'Make a copy,' she asked Nilly.

'During the break,' he promised. 'I don't want to disrupt the class now.'

'Make a copy,' she asked, again. 'Tell C. to make a copy.'

When she asked him a few times, Nilly went inside to make one. They were both class disruptors now, but she absolutely had to know right now, what's what and why she was there. The copy was black and white, not in colour, but otherwise looked the same.

'What did he say?' the girl asked.

'Who?'

'Him. C.'

'He said you don't need it,' Nilly said, convincingly.

When the date was stamped on the top of the page, it was time to start 'work'. What a sound the stamping machine made! The only other thing Nilly could think of, that made a similar sound, was a punching machine, also used on the premises. It was used to make holes in a stack of paper sheets, that were then bound together, using a plastic ring. One could, actually, buy notebooks, in which sheets of paper of the same or very similar size had already holes in them, and all hung on a ring, to make it easy flipping through them, adding and removing pages. Why wasn't this a suitable object for student work? How much time and punching effort it could save a teacher? But nothing doing, you can think so as much as you want, but they still made all the notebooks themselves, using an old-school, as C. has put it, punching machine.

When did corporal punishment stop being used in Australian schools? Nilly asked himself, but realized, that he didn't know. How little he actually did know of their history. The teacher couldn't actually remember it, from the time when he was already working in schools, or could he? He wasn't sure.

When the date stamp was finished with, they started working. The work was cutting out all alphabet letters from a sheet of paper, and gluing vowels, all five of them, together, on a red star. The twenty-one consonants went together on another shape, a blue oval. Nilly shook his head, repeatedly, trying not to see an egg in it, but couldn't. A big blue egg. Did they mean it? And if not, what did they mean? The girl, it appeared, did not know any letters, whatsoever. No wonder, if all consonants go together on a blue oval. Like they all consent to something blue, and nauseatingly elongated. Did they mean it? And if not, what did they mean?

She didn't know any letters, no doubt about it, but always stumbled a bit longer over y. Is it a vowel? A consonant? Nilly turned the page, and found they had to do it all again. Glue the vowels together, on a star, consonants together, on an oval. But this time y was a vowel, too. Whoever made it, Nilly thought, must've asked himself the same question. Is Y a vowel? And if not, what is it? A big or small yus? If it is, however, a vowel, Nilly went on, there are words out there, which have four vowels in them. Yo-yo, for example. Anything else? Thinking about other such words, he looked around. He felt he really needed to share his thoughts on vowels with somebody.

A yo-yo makes you think of depression, bipolar and all that. But the girl wasn't depressed. She looked so calm. But wasn't allowed inside. Why was that?

It was time for lunch now. People went outside and sat around the table where the girl's coloured pencils and workbook and flash cards were all piled at the centre. Somebody told her it was food time. 'Not for me,' she said. Was it, perhaps, because some of these people were allowed, now and then, to buy a coffee from a café, and she couldn't do it, since she had no money? Was she simply so appalled with everything she saw, that she couldn't think of food? But chips in a bowl and salsa in a small cup appeared, nevertheless, on the table. She was now writing in missing letters in some words on the page. Bed, zip and fan, Nilly read. There was something else. She absolutely didn't know, what has to be inserted in the middle of each, although she didn't, actually, look stupid. Was it because all twenty-one consonants went together on a blue oval, and there were simply too many? And on top of it, Y was nobody knows what, and when it was a vowel, twenty consonants went together? Did she simply see all these zips and fans as offensive, although and because she couldn't read it?

Somebody asked her again, if she wanted to eat something. She was eating chips already, but it wasn't enough.

And then she threw down an empty chair, that stood next to her, on the floor.

'I threw it for you,' she said, to somebody. Nilly opened his mouth to say he's never seen her to do something like that. It was true. But there must be a reason, after all, why she was where she was. If she absolutely couldn't be tolerated in the room with other people, because you can't put up with somebody throwing chairs and stuff, that would be a valid reason. It would have explained it.

Nilly decided he's had enough. Somebody has to pick up what she was throwing, and if he stays, that will be him. Did they mean it? And if not, what did they mean?

'Do you know what minimal pairs are?' he asked the teacher, C. He looked completely blank. No sign of recognition.

'Minimal pairs,' Nilly repeated. 'Like cat-pat-mat, pot-cot-tot? They help to show a student what letters are for. Have you heard of them?'

He received no answer and made his way out. Minimal pairs can't be more important, that the rest of that shit, but somehow Nilly found it most vexing. He hasn't heard of minimal pairs. What can you expect? How can it be, really?

LA PARURE

Tu dis que tu as acheté une rivière de diamants pour remplacer la mienne?

- Oui. Tu ne t'en etais pas aperçue, hein? Elles etaient bien pareilles.

Et elle souriait d'une joie orgueilleuse et naïve.

- Mais la mienne etait fausse. Elle valait au plus cinq cents francs!... (Guy de Maupassant. La parure.)

Kira looked again at the text projected on the wall. A case study.

'Ashley is an intellectually disabled adult. Jay and Jack are both support workers working with Ashley. Jack noticed that Jay often touches Ashley, and Ashley doesn't like it. What should Jack do? What would you do in this situation?'

Kira felt she was getting red and hot. For a minute or two she was rehearsing what she'd say. 'It's rude. I've known somebody whose name was this,' she finally squeezed out. 'And my own last name is Jay. You can't have names of the people in the audience in your case studies.'

The woman took a pause. She eyed Kira and was thinking about what to say, obviously.

'Do you think Jay and Ashley are males or females? How is it different if Jay is male? If Ashley is male? Female?' she said. Kira was silent. It made a difference, of course. And she didn't know what else to say, anyway.

'The right word for this crap is misogyny,' Kira thought. 'Males or females Jay and Ashley, misogyny it is. Really. They must hate you to tell something like this. And all these names which can be either, really, is just a very thin camouflage. She's known three Ashleys and two Jays, and they were all males.

'But anyway...by the way', she went on, 'there must be a few different kinds of that damn thing, misogyny. At least three. Mi[s]ogyny, mi[z]ogyny and missisogyny. If it's your looks they most object to, it's misogyny with an [s]. If it's what you can do, it's mi[z]ogyny with a [z]. And the worst kind is, in my opinion, missisogyny. It's the least talked about, that's why not everybody knows about it. The worst of all. When your boss goes 'Sheilah, how much your partner is earning, it's twice as much as I do,' it's missisogyny. But one thing doesn't necessarily exclude the other. You can always pick and mix. If they object to the way you look, they simply don't let you do some things, and you never can do them. No mi[z]ogyny, then? 'I'm confused,' she thought. 'But anyway, the good thing is that if you aren't making any money at all, ultimately you won't have too much to spend on body care and clothes. So your looks will be satisfactory.'

Kira shook her head and tried to think of something else. On the other hand, what do they do? Themselves? What can they do?

Take this woman, for example. Right now she was telling a group of students about teaching people with an intellectual disability to read. For some mysterious reason she wanted to see the phonic approach implemented all the time. Why phonics? Who knows.

Somebody must have told her some time ago it's a good thing. Or was it her subconscious playing? Just because it starts with an [f]? She seemed interested in things like this.

'But seriously,' Kira thought. 'How much does she know about the phonics? For example, if you ask her what's the difference between a phoneme, a sound, and a letter, what would she say? What about all two-letter combinations, like –ea– and –ee– and –oi– and –oo? Does she know they can be the same phoneme? If people can read them in meaningless words, they know the rules, although not necessarily can tell what they are, if you ask them. If people read slower, when the word is an invented one, like 'fean', they know the rules, but in a normal context rely on a sentence. On what it means.

'Well, not quite,' she corrected herself. 'Real words can be recognized faster, because they are more familiar, than invented ones, and therefore it takes less time. If a meaningful context speeds it up further, it means it's easier to read words in a sentence. And words like 'fean' are all different too. Some look more real and are based on frequently occurring letter-combinations in them. They must be easier to read, than, say, 'chaifhsity'. And word length must be a factor, too. '

She thought a bit more and realized that word length is either more or less important than word familiarity. These two things may interact, too: the importance of familiarity is different for words of different length. And that somebody must have looked at it, she just doesn't know. And that it can be different for different people. And maybe even different languages, with more and less phonetic spelling systems. Generally, however, word length and familiarity go together: really rare words are longer ones. But not necessarily: take 'everyone', for example. Actually all three – familiarity, word length, and a meaningful context, best of all, funny and easy to remember – are important. And you only have to have a hint of an attention problem to function better, if you see colourful pictures. Especially the ones you like. That's why Dr Seuss is so beautiful. But they don't use it. Instead they use black and white flash cards. And by the way, lots of similar-sounding words, like pot and hot, and cat and mat promote the phonic awareness. Like nothing else, including flash cards, and much easier.'

Kira tried to understand what the woman would think and say about it.

'But these people, the disabled, are taught quite differently. They are taught to read single words out of context first. And often never graduate to normal, even simple ones, texts. Because it's seen as more difficult. Instead they talk about phonics to her. And like centipedes, asked which foot he puts first, stumble. Is it why it's done, to make the speediest ones think about what they do when they walk?'

'She doesn't have to know all about phonics,' Kira thought. 'Although it probably helps, if you know there is something to know here. But really, you don't have to know it. Intuition and good will, lots of it, much more than this woman has, is probably enough.'

The problem is not that she is undereducated in things she wants to talk about,' Kira decided. 'Although maybe it matters too. The problem is that she doesn't want them to learn, as far as I can see. Somebody who hasn't heard about phonics at all would be better. And by the way, it is like reading. I'm literate, although not really well-read in the subject of phonics. But she is simply illiterate.'

'But anyway, what does she know?' Kira decided to find out and ask a question.

'What's the difference,' she said, and all the rest of it. About the context that speeds up or slows the reading process. 'Single words are far more abstract,' she said. 'Why is it that if somebody has a difficulty, we make them do a more abstract task?'

There was no answer for a while. The woman was thinking. When she started to speak, it was something which had no real meaning, Kira thought. Matching. Matching written and printed words was the answer. 'If students can match, it'll help,' the woman said.

'But can they read handwriting? Do they understand what matching is,' Kira thought. She decided she shouldn't argue anymore, and didn't say anything. You have to show people what matching is first, but by the time they get it, they are sure they can't do it.

Although of course they can, if you want them to. Like everything. What about this old question, however: if you want to know how much jungle people know, do you start by making them match geometric forms? Probably not. They say not. Although, of course, if somebody can read, they must be able to match circles with circles and so on. Because letters are more complex forms. Is it true, actually? Especially these days, when text is everywhere, and lots of things are ...what d'you call it? Interactive? You won't get your lunch unless you send a text and order. People are simply much more exposed to all things written, than, say, two hundred years ago. No wonder their reading skills are different. But they want it to be the same. For some mysterious reason, not being able to read and write is still the main proof of stupidity. They want a proof.'

'I can see you know your stuff,' the woman said. 'Come up here. Tell us all about it.'

'Next time,' Kira muttoned. She felt scared. She didn't expect this at all.

Then there was something else and again something else. More case studies. Other people's lives decomposed and deconstructed and fancied and fantasized about for the sake of... What exactly it was the sake of, Kira wasn't sure. Could it be some kind of gluttony? You feel hungry and thirsty for details, real or not. And this is just a sophisticated form of gossip. A more advanced and acceptable one. And, most importantly, paid for as part of your employment. Called case studies. The only difference is that if you don't want to do gossip, you don't have to. But the only way not to listen to this is to disappear. A kind of rape, really. A mental one. On the other hand, if the woman was talking about phonics, she'd have to do some homework, and it would take her time and effort, too.

'The strange thing is,' Kira realized, suddenly, 'that apparently nobody told her that one can have case studies in learning to read, too. And it even makes more sense. Because you can generalize, of course, about how it happens, but there are limits. Lots of things fall outside of them. And maybe the most interesting ones.'

'God, what a bitch she is,' Kira thought. 'Can be either a man or a woman. If Jay is a man and Ashley a woman, is it better or worse? What about the other way round? And if you think you know what man it is, you are dead wrong. They have a woman with exactly the same name in one of their groups. And a very similar incident had happened to her in the past. Maybe even was recorded. Not a big deal. Disabled don't matter as much as somebody else to whom otherwise it could be hinting.'

'But really,' Kira wanted to think something good now. Uplifting. 'It's completely crazy. These people are taught not to touch under any circumstances. They just wave their hands in the air and it means a hug to them. And they still get abused in all sorts of back rooms and in most cases don't dare speak about it.

But everybody else is talking their heads off. And not just talk. They kiss when they meet, kiss when they say goodbye. It's normal. Although these hungry for touch people, the disabled, aren't allowed it. Social kissing, that is. And not just kissing. There exists such a thing as social fucking, practiced in many advanced environments. Talked about as calmly as if it was...if it was... As if it was shaking hands.'

'Anyway, would it be right to conclude that it means nothing now? Like shaking hands? Like social kissing? But not at all. Firstly, because there are some people who aren't allowed it. The disabled, for example. If everybody can have something, it has no value. Even monkeys know it. The alpha monkey can have what others can't. The point is not to let everybody have it, or it gets so bland. And secondly, because nobody knows what they believe. 'It's time to ask yourself what you believe.' Who said it? They don't ask. If you ask, you get some kind of answer, and it all becomes simply boring. It's better not to know. Not to ask if social kissing and social fucking is OK, and who exactly it is meant to be for. The next case study will show. Really if it's not OK, it's just the old way, and it's tedious. And if it is OK, it's just as tedious, because everything is possible and there are no inhibitions to break. It's much more interesting if you don't know. You can always play with it then.

Kira couldn't remember how much she said of all this. The training workshop was over, at last. She walked to the station and popped into a jewelry shop. It sold unusual interesting pieces, made of thread, cord and fabric. She put one on, and accidentally tore it. Mi[s]ogyny, mi[z]ogyny and missisogyny. It was the first time she realized that there are three.

The owner made her promise she'll come back and pay for it. But she never did.

Lisa
A novel

1.

Where has she gone wrong? Lisa was still looking for mistakes, although she couldn't tell if it helps. She didn't mean helps every day. Of course it did, somehow. But did it help on a large scale? Looking for mistakes, she thought, is where what we believe in shows up. The unnecessary, like an old leaf, falls off and the truth appears. If not the truth, maybe something like it?

The truth infused with a bitter experience. Or the other way round: experience infused with truth? Trying to decide what's infused with what and whether it has to be bitter – Lisa remembered that when somebody, usually it was her mother, asked her about a friend or a common acquaintance if she got married, Lisa would become angry. She would talk endlessly, often in rage, and felt herself that she was both aggressive and thirsty for revenge. But she couldn't stop. She tried to explain that nobody – just nobody, believe it or not, - does live this way anymore. Not anymore – do you hear me? What she meant was – if somebody pushed me, even a little bit, not that it matters now, I'm not going to do it to somebody else – because I'm so much better and altogether different. She sounded, she thought, just crazy – at times, when she would stop and hear herself – she could feel it. What was it about, really? Revenge? Was telling old people that they are not up to date revenge? She didn't want, in fact, to see it clearly. Although there was – she was sure of it – something not quite commonplace about the whole situation. Say it? Not now, she decided, maybe later, certainly later. But in the meantime... In the meantime, she had to understand what mistakes she'd made. And why. A straight A student was her very essence. But who cares? A good student was all there was at the bottom of it, and she was not the only one like this. Scary, the whole thing. All she was taught was rubbish at best. Yes. But nothing doing now, she had to look for mistakes. To find the root of it, to start at the beginning. But why the beginning? She could start anywhere, it is not what matters.

But the golden cat, the one Tashka and Lisa spoke about, she was there. Just a short while ago. It wasn't, she thought, the most gracious animal on Earth, but ... And all for what? She'll get there. If she is looking for mistakes, she has to start at some important point. Where?

2.

The Queen's Market was an ideal place, from Lisa's point of view, for a night out. There was everything: lots of loud music and a crowd of differently accented people in the middle of which only a five-legged person – or a very lazy one – wouldn't feel like they are belonging. Lisa felt, at times, like a five-legged one, but not, she realized, quite to this extent. Not enough. It was a question, of course, if belonging still meant something for a crowd like this. And definitely not the same thing as it did in Moscow kitchens. 'Doesn't matter, don't get sucked in there,' she told herself. There was lots of different food, which, to her felt like unusual and interesting. The best thing was, however, noise. It was like a curtain, Lisa thought, nobody paid too much attention to you because of it and you could always hide behind it. And feel safe. Or, maybe, the best thing was not the noise. Because there were many other good things. She was eating hurriedly a spicy potato twist from a wooden skewer and thinking all the time about her new shoes. The shoes she had on were new and too tight, they've already blistered her feet. Lisa tried to walk in little steps, carefully, to avoid further injury. There was a lot to look at – a huge craft market and all the food stalls.

And the thoughts were blistering, too. One had to be an idiot, Lisa thought, not to learn something like this over all these years. I could be at peace with people and myself, just think of it. She loved all these weaved baskets from the Pacific – what was it called, exactly? - cosmetic bags from used toothpaste tubes, all kinds of shiny and not too expensive jewellery, including the most unthinkable-looking, even the witch hats. She couldn't tell if they were made from dry herb or wire – but who cares? – tried them on. All the time at the back of her mind was a scratching thought that she's just a kind of outsider, an admiring consumer who can't do anything like this – pity. Well, maybe she could, a little bit. But to sell it was a totally different matter. One had to know a lot...She wasn't quite sure of what precisely...But definitely a lot...Her lot was, obviously, to be a Soviet all her life. Or was it, maybe, all because it wasn't as high-brow and interesting to her as some other things? Science? Maybe, she suddenly realized, she was just under K's influence; he has always called all these crafty things and pastimes, with no exception, 'handicarves'. A kind of mockery, subtle or not so subtle. To be caught 'handicarving' would be humiliating. But what kind of honest – why honest, just a reasonable one – person blames his own silly mistakes and inertia on other people? Wasn't it what she was doing? What's that saying? A bad dancer is trapped by his own balls?

There was a dancer, too, by the way, and not a bad one. How different her state of mind was from K's has become most obvious while they were watching him. The dancer was blond and has been middle-aged for some time now – at least ten years – Lisa thought. To the sound of a guitar, which was the first thing you could hear, coming close, and to something else that Lisa couldn't see – he jumped and did various dainty – that's the word, she decided – pas. He waved his arms in the air, as if he was stroking an invisible woman. Did half and full turns on one foot and jumped, rather high for a street show. All slightly exaggerated, good-humoured stuff. Lisa found it funny, but K., apparently, didn't. The shoes were tight and kept blistering her feet, but sangria, sold for eight dollars for a big plastic vessel at the door, was beautiful. Lisa decided that she hadn't tasted anything better, perhaps. Even the ice-cubes that clinked in it didn't bother her, although usually she asked for no ice in all drinks she had.

The street show reminded her of something, but she couldn't quite catch what. 'In a sense,' she thought, 'it's like my relationship with my mother-tongue. Especially recently. No more no less. I always feel a bit unreal now when I come to Moscow. I can't believe that people around me can understand everything I say. It's so unusual. I forget about it, and become arrogant, almost rude. I can ask loudly, if there are many tajiks in town. Maybe I just suppress the knowledge that they can understand me? because it's an unpleasant one? But why should it be unpleasant? Is it because I'm too much like them, in fact, in my other life? I even feel like if I have no accent, it's almost accidental. A strange coincidence. You can bring a child anywhere for a year or two, and in the end of this time, he will speak whatever it is they speak there. For life. The memory of the place itself may disappear, but not this strange camouflage of words. It'll stay. I want to be like this child,' Lisa thought. 'But I'm not, of course. But for some reason I feel like I can speak the language of my childhood only to some. The family, and, maybe, a few other people. It's not quite transferable.'

'Another thing is,' Lisa liked all kinds of similarities and analogies and always looked for them with pleasure, 'another thing is that it all reminds me of mixing drinks. Why not mix everything with everything else? They mix vodka with orange juice. Almost everybody. And it can be even worse. Why not add to it, vodka and juice, that is, some coffee liquor? Maybe it is a bad taste and a dreadful combination, but tastes can be different. Everybody knows this. Try and prove positively that it tastes bad.

Suddenly she remembered a scrap of an old conversation. Just a formula that stuck in her memory. Try... Or was it experience?... try on different forms of marriage. And they said that not everybody can afford it. Which was, evidently, not a good thing at all. Why not vodka and coffee liquor then? One has to get used to everything to appreciate it. But not too much used, just a little bit, because, after some time, you get fed up with everything. Even vodka and orange juice with coffee liquor. She looked at the dancer again and sighed. Maybe, not quite naturally. It's not surprising that she finds it funny. Somebody else could be disgusted. Or offended. But, again, we become offended only by things which have something to do with us. Relevant, in a sense. 'I'm making circles,' Lisa thought and had another sip of cold sangria. She couldn't, maybe, explain, why she was making circles every time she thought of it, but she felt she was. She got distracted, but there was more than a half of a plastic- what d'you call it? A cup? A glass? – left.

Yes, mix vodka and orange juice and add a bit of beer. She was feeling all the time how much better sangria was. Maybe, it just seems so? People are looking at the dancer and nobody is laughing. Nor frowning. 'The belief that's shared by nobody is called schizophrenia.' This piece of wisdom belongs to somebody well-known. If everybody can see one tree and you're seeing two, there must be something wrong with your sight. Seeing double. Or just drunk. But everybody is drinking sangria here. Who knows what they see, and why, and how many? Thinking of schizophrenia, Lisa also thought of something – was it a paper she heard delivered? – recently. It was about a rather well-known Russian poetess who died in a psychiatric clinic. The speaker tried to translate her. It turned out, surprisingly, that it wasn't easy. There were too many untranslatable words, bits and pieces. There were two thoughts in Lisa's head: I will end up like her, in a psychiatric something, and another one: why is it that I absolutely can't to – what d'you call it? – get along? adapt? – to all of this? The academic system? Even the woman who spoke on the poetess and obvious difficulties translating her, could do it better. But why? Really, why?

There were a few reasons, Lisa thought, but she wasn't sure which one is the most important. If you don't know, it means, there is none. But... The first one was, of course, the emigration. Or immigration, if you look at it from the other side. She's never been an expert in - what's the best way to put it? - in human interaction, but here... Here it's all become different. Especially, at first. But why should one be a genius, a guru, or whatever... in getting along with strange people, if all you want is to be allowed to water and cultivate your little scholarly paddock? Nonsense. Maybe, it's simply not true? But it was, she was convinced that it was.

It shouldn't be necessary. But it was. You can't get anywhere without it. And, maybe, even more importantly – humanities people have different norms in life – they are, themselves, like of another culture. She firmly believed in this piece of questionable wisdom, that she read in a book a very long time ago. Humanities people are different. But she was different too – made of another type of clay. Both her parents were engineers . There is simply more space there, and everything is simpler. And better. Especially people. Why is it simpler and better, Lisa, maybe, wouldn't be able to tell, but she was convinced that it was true. Simpler and better, because people are better, more honest, maybe. Just a different type of people. And she must be just a wrong type – knocking on the wrong door. Why did it happen, at all? Maybe, because she was interested in the subject matter. Or just accidentally. There is a fashion for everything. And she wanted so much to be different from her parents. And what – a mess, yes, that's the word – it is now.

3.

But it didn't all happen at once. At first Lisa was employed in a Nii, which was an abbreviation for a 'scientific research institute'. Everything, or almost everything, where no manual labour was done, was called this. Although it was a scientific research institute, it was not considered 'academic', a contradiction hard to explain, and there wasn't much prestige in the whole thing either. The institute was called 'agricultural' and she was slightly ashamed of this. Patents or library work would be better – not so shameful at all. But agriculture? No. There was something clearly not 'comme il faut' about the whole thing. At least, this was not 'comme il faut' and slightly embarassing from the point of view of a certain 'milieu' which she belonged to. Not everything which wasn't quite within the framework of, say, your university major was mauvais ton, but agriculture clearly was. She couldn't tell why, and hardly anybody else could. Maybe, the reason was that 'food packages' – that you could buy weekly at the institute at a rather low price and that you'd never find in a regular shop – were too good there. And the cantine. All honest intelligentsia was chasing food, especially 'deficit', lacking in ordinary suburban shops and queuing for hours, and at this difficult time she could just buy what she wanted in her agricultural institute. Definitely not 'comme il faut'. At least, from the point of view of people like her parents. Lisa suspected even then that people who worked in humanities would have a different attitude towards 'food packages'. And how acceptable this was. But only suspected, no certainty at all. Just maybe. It was a distant acquaintance – one of her parents' - who recommended her this institute. Not because of food packages, of course. But because they promised two 'library days', when she didn't have to be in the office. Lisa's daughter was just two then, and it mattered a lot to her.

'I can't promise, Lisotchka, that you will have one free day a week regularly, but two also won't be a problem, if necessary,' the future boss Semen Aronovitch told her, when they first met.

Lisa was so inexperienced then that she concluded, from this strangely-shaped phrase, that everything will be the way she wanted it to be. Maybe because she had no choice. It turned out later that she was too shy to ask even for one free day a week, let alone two. After she'd asked for two once – he said himself it shouldn't be a problem, didn't he – Lisa realized that it's impossible to do it every week, however much she'd like to. 'Has something happened, Lisotchka? Is everything all right at home?' Semen asked and lifted his brows. 'But anyway, if you need it, you sure will have it.'

From then on, Lisa took a sick day, whenever she needed a free one, which was, more or less, all the time. It was simpler – she'd always get a few days at once, minimum three, and there was no humiliation of asking. Maybe, she just didn't know how to ask otherwise. The sick days were paid for only at fifty percent level, because she just started working then, and her service time, which was the thing that mattered in this case, was zero. But Lisa didn't think it mattered much. K. earned enough already, and all in all, she didn't think halving her pay for a week or two was problematic, even if an extra cup of coffee didn't always seem within her reach then. Sick-day certificates always decorated her bookshelf in those days – and coming back to Semen she didn't always take them to payroll – it seemed safer not to attract too much attention – or was it just that she didn't care?

What could be squeezed between sick day certificates? Not much work maybe, but they say there is always a place for romance. It was in this agricultural institute that Lisa has had what was, perhaps, the most interesting almost -happened-love story of her life. The most interesting one, of course, not counting those very early ones which she had before she got married at twenty. They were, Lisa firmly believed, something very special. Much more interesting, than anything that happened or could have happened later. All of them, as such, just by virtue of the time when it happened. And, maybe, place? Yes, more interesting than anything that happened or could have happened later. It was her attitude. Something like a habit of conscience. It was hard to say now when she's acquired it: probably, as a child. Or ten years later when some things became so habitual that she couldn't pay any more attention to them.

'It's two o'clock!' her mother almost shouted.

'I said I will be back late. And left a note.'

'You leave this note every day.'

'So what?'

'What do you mean so what? It should mean something.'

'It does.'

Or was it that Lisa was too much impressed, when she first heard her mum talking breathlessly about a Romeo and Juliet film: it was filmed in the real age, fourteen or something like it, and this was the most interesting thing about it.

Like all important habits of conscience, with time she started doubting it, and looking for reasons, but it was too late. The conscience was where it was. The habit was already there. But most strongly she was doubting it, maybe (Lisa noticed that she put 'maybe' in the middle of every sentence, but couldn't get rid of it), just once. In those long-forgotten far-away days of her affair with the Soviet agricultural bureaucracy. The blessed agricultural Nii with its numerous special kiosks, selling much better meat, than your average suburban shop, cheaper, but better coffee shops and other well-hidden interesting outlets. They had a beautiful age difference, Lisa thought, it mattered to her, about eight years or so. Lisa was twenty four, and a bit over thirty seemed like a lot to her. Unlike Lisa, who was called a 'senior economist' and paid just over a hundred roubles – a minimum wage – he has moved on up this strange agricultural quasi-research ladder quite enough by then. And was paid accordingly. A reason to show some respect, if not to imitate the behaviour, after all. A ladder which in this particular case was decorated with unexpectedly, for Lisa, who never expected any such thing, complicated frills. Like 'senior' added to the status of somebody who was a student just yesterday.

He's moved up that ladder and was paid quite a lot, according to the then and there standards. And at the same time had what you'd call some other serious interests. Like theatre. The theatre was considered an amateur one then, but was counted among the most interesting ones in town. They often talked about it. Or rather, he talked, and Lisa listened, or showed that she listened. Showed, because she felt, all the time, that she had to emphasize it a bit. Who knows why? Maybe, because she didn't quite feel what she was supposed to? Or quite the opposite? Anyway, the emphasized listening made the whole thing feel a bit theatrical. Soon the amateur theatre shed its amateur status, like a snake does an old skin. And around this time –maybe, just a couple of months later – he left the country. Decided not to go with the new professionals into the new and the unknown.

There was, of course, the new and the unknown, but it was all about the emigration. The new and the unknown fitted nicely within the frame and habits of this circle – fuzzily defined but real – of Nii workers aspiring to achieve more. That Lisa just joined.

Also, the new 'market prices', rising daily, were not the last thing to consider. But it was so nice in the very beginning of perestroika – when nobody has learned yet when, and where, and how much. And for how long. They talked about life and theatre, while Lisa was smoking near a staircase outside the room where she sat with about a dozen of other people. She smoked a few times a day, to brighten up what felt like eight hours of daily prison. But not on library days: thank God for a kind boss!

There, near the staircase, they were once found by a middle-aged woman who sat in the same, very full with people, room with Lisa. The woman went out to smoke too – her white bleached hair was peppered with ash - she did it every hour, perhaps.

'I think Semen has a girlfriend somewhere,' he was saying.

'Why?'

'Somebody's calling all the time. A woman I don't know.'

'It's his wife.' Lisa wanted her to be his wife. 'What's she doing, by the way?'

'Spending time somewhere nine to five. More or less for nothing.'

'Where?'

'I don't know. I've always thought, by the way, that my wife won't need it.'

'Does she?'

'Well... you know...'

The bleached woman took in the whole scene with one short stare – both seemed too much involved into the conversation – and smiled. It was a sinister smile, Lisa thought. Two weeks later Lisa gave up smoking at work – and a short time afterwards anywhere – they found that she had a weak heart and her breath would become wheezy and difficult after just one cigarette. It was hard to go up the stairs to the common room, where she sat, after this: she couldn't breathe.

So it didn't happen. Not even when Semen – what could he mean – sent them together to a conference to a smallish Ukranian town. Lisa was reimbursed for the tickets there and didn't need anything else, since she stayed with somebody she knew from long time ago. She was told that she doesn't have to attend the conference at all, and found it, maybe, slightly offending, but at the same time, pleasantly liberating: if she didn't have to attend it, there was much more time to see the city and to switch from home. There were some friends living here, and some friends' friends. Somebody agreed to show her around. Maybe, she was shy of them? It was, after all, an observant, and observing eye?

When in the second morning of the four days they had for the trip he called her to tell he was sick and asked to come and see him for – there should have been a 'for', but what was it? – she came. Of course she did, when higher-standing comrades asked her to. Or, maybe, there was no trace of this 'higher-standing' flavour whatsoever – did it matter? A bright red dress she wore was her favourite since a long time before, perhaps, since her second or third year at uni. But nothing happened, maybe, because Lisa didn't quite realize, straight away, what was supposed to. She's always been a little bit naïve, even much later. This was, perhaps, the secret to her – was 'charm' the right word? she wondered – it must be - in later years. She didn't quite get what kind of sickness it was, but she's always been compassionate, always.

Nothing helped, not even the sale of 'deficit', not found in regular retail, footwear in their agricultural Nii. Normally they had one held monthly (or, if they were a bit less lucky – bi-monthly; what it depended on, had always been a subject of much speculation). This was when Lisa met his wife. The wife, for some reason, was like the last, all-deciding argument to Lisa. She was a brightly-coloured, beautiful woman, with a little bit Eastern appearance. She also came from somewhere in Ukraine. She was around thirty then, noticeably, crucially older, than Lisa, but also quite young, by the Western standards. What was she thinking? Who knows. Maybe, nothing at all? She just knew that it can't be, and that was it. Or, maybe, the reason for it all was a child, her son, a rather difficult child, they said. Lisa didn't want the child to be hers, not in any sense. And the woman... For a long time, if not always, she would be unhappy. Lisa didn't doubt that the woman will be unhappy, how could she? Not for a moment. But what for? Or why? For their long conversations about life and against bureaucracy? Because Lisa is younger and more beautiful? But what if some day somebody... She shook off this unpleasant thought and decided that the 'don't steal' commandment is carved in stone. How else? It all is. Don't judge and you won't be. Don't steal and... what should it be? You won't be? You won't be from? What if, however, she can think it all only because she has all the same as this black-curls doll? Does it matter, why? No. She paid for the winter boots, a real find, natural leather, a comfortable, sensible heel and said good-bye. The footwear thing was finished, thank God.

4.

Two years have gone and her dream has come true: Lisa was now working in what was called, then, the Academy. That is, in a research institute, a Nii, that belonged to this blessed and still sufficiently funded body: the academy. It's taken some asking for – not hers, of course, she was just a girl, but the whole family was interested in her not having to attend somewhere every day. It saved some babysitting strain.

And finally, it happened: the happiness of prestige and free, as they called it, attendance. Prettier than ever before, Lisa looked as if within her was a permanently shining lamp. The nanny who used to come twice a week was almost unnecessary now. Both grandmas became much happier and suddenly remembered that they were working, too, and, maybe most importantly, had some interests of their own, and hobbies. Since Lisa changed jobs, her mum had more time to play piano in the evening, and to study languages. Wasn't it all logical, even blissfully so?

'I think it suits you, Lisa, you look so much better now,' her then supervisor, 'Shefinia', as Lisa called her, would say. They were walking the streets of Moscow, just for fun. Strangely, Lisa realized that it's never happened before. Maybe, they were both too pressed for time?

Lisa's connection with Shefinia was informal. They met when Lisa was in her third year, by chance: somebody's introduced Lisa because she was so much interested in all things psychological. Shefinia supervised Lisa's 'kursoviks', that is, undergraduate research, a few years in a row, and published it all with a certain small press. It mattered a lot to her – these edited collections of students' and other, often non-student, papers. Lisa just followed her attitude, in a sense: if somebody she respected so much said it mattered, then it did. And if they said it mattered a lot, however unexpected it can be, it must be true, too.

The connection was purely informal, until Lisa graduated and entered what was called 'zaochnaia aspirantura': a distance graduate school. Her nationality, they said, the 'fifth question' (what, she wondered, was the questionnaire that has given this name to the whole thing? When?) wouldn't let her enter a normal, the so-called 'day' one instead. There could be other reasons, too, but this was a satisfactory one. But the distance school was a good one as well.

It allowed her to apply for one free day a week, on a permanent basis, while she still worked in her agricultural institute, with its brutally early start time and soothingly cheap and delicious meat pies sold in every corner, that you could calm yourself with, once you were there. Also, the distance grad school entitled her to an additional month of a paid leave in summer. Supposedly, she would use it to prepare for examinations. There were none, actually, after she was in, but who cares? To have two months in summer, instead of one, justified everything. Not to have to come to the agricultural Nii every day was a pure bliss.

How often during the last year and a half Lisa would run in at 8.45 and drink, like other people, a cup of tea in her seat, immediately. Trying to figure out at the same time, what they were busy with. And then realize, again, that she doesn't have enough energy, nor patience, nor interest in understanding it. And thank God, it's unnecessary: Semen granted her complete freedom within the required office hours. The important thing was to come in time and to signal her presence with a bag on top of the table. And once it's done, one could choose what to do. If you can't choose, there are other options: go to the library for the whole day, bring your own books, since the library was, of course, agricultural, and create: write your articles for those print-on-demand published by another institute collections, as long as you can. But often she felt she couldn't drag herself through the whole day, from nine in the morning till six, when they were allowed to leave, especially when she took her attention away from a white sheet of paper and thought of other things. Like try to estimate as well as she could what she could buy at the supermarket with the coins in her pocket – one pack of pelmeni, or, maybe, take two? – and at how many minutes past seven she will be home, if there is a queue at the supermarket. And what if she'll drink a coffee at lunch inside the agricultural institute, or maybe have another one at five? It's such an awfully long time till six!

'The way you live is called inner emigration,' her friend at the agricultural institute told her. 'Pure escapism.'

'I don't know,' Lisa said. 'What's inner emigration? It sounds like a HR document. Or a party meeting.'

'It's obvious. You're escaping Semen and all these ladies in your room upstairs. But they won't let it pass, just like this.'

'The ladies rather than Semen. I like him. But why do you think they won't 'let it pass?''

'They'll make you pay. Maybe not right now.'

''How?'

'I don't know. But they will.'

'It's not true about emigration. I don't want to leave. And my parents never will.'

'Why?'

'They like it here. But you know,' Lisa added as an afterthought, 'the ladies aren't all against me.'

'No?'

'I had tea with Lydia yesterday in the morning and she told me she'd quit it all, if only there was somebody who'd pay her monthly even a small sum, like a hundred rubles. She said it was her dream.'

Lydia was a smart-looking brunette in her thirties, a 'kandidat nauk' already, that is, with a degree, and a senior researcher on a good salary. Lisa sat next to her in the room, often watched her, puzzled, nobody knew what by, and stopped only when she caught herself staring too hard.

'She doesn't mean it,' he said, 'but even if she does, what makes you think she's on your side, saying this?'

'She means it or she doesn't?'

Lisa's mood went down when she thought that, indeed, she was sitting nobody knows where and doing nobody knows what: who of all these people sharing the space with her could be interested in the nature of psychological association? All these links, often suddenly emerging in one's memory: house – building- townhouse – cottage – hut – granny flat – skyscraper – shed – block of flats.

'Cottage is not a Russian word,' Lisa thought. But, just theoretically speaking, perhaps they could be interested? Probably yes, but why? And what would be their response? She wanted to try and see, but this happened only when she was asked what she was doing in her 'distance grad school'. Not very often. More often, instead of trying, she would go and call Shefinia from a phone booth on the first floor. And hear, usually, that all science – she intoned 'all science' in a strange, slightly foreign way, raising the voice on the second word, - all science functions like this, Lisa. Especially pure one, as opposed to applied. If you have twenty, or fifteen readers, it's a success, really. And the next collection of articles, in which they all appear, will be published in a few months. And Lisa felt better. Everything had its reason, after all. It occurred to her later, that all her doubts were primed, as psychologists say, by uneasy thoughts about stretching the time and money to buy a second pack of pelmeni, and then stretching it all a bit more, to be able to make her babysitter's fortnightly payment. All this was, in a sense, accidental, that is, having little to do with the matter itself: in this case, the nature of associative links between nouns denoting different kinds of structures erected by humans. Buildings, to put it simply. Although, of course, while they lived with her parents, for the first year and a half, it has been much easier. But anyway, all this was a kind of a confounding factor, an interference, like priming a reaction time by something else. Her perception of it all, Semen, his Nii and the ladies has been primed with the work start time and the transport, the end time and the wretched pelmeni, and, most of all, with her babysitter's difficult character. It must be like this for everybody, but Lisa thought, suddenly, that Shefinia can't understand. She has always been single, a woman in her late fifties now, childless and completely free.

5.

So the new life was better than the previous one in all respects, but, most importantly, because it allowed flexible hours. Each week, she had to attend on two days, Tuesday and Thursday, and one more day, the third one, everybody could choose as they liked. On the other two 'library' days they were supposed to work at home. What was it, if not happiness itself. And no need to ask for it. Her new boss Olga was not at all like her Shefinia. Twenty years younger and made, as they say, of a totally different dough. Lexicography, she said, is not really science. It's rather a practical kind of craft, which makes it acceptable. As for science as such, Olga said, women are not really meant to do it. She herself was not really meant to do it. They would have long conversations on the subject now and then. Most of them started with Olga's generalized statements. Lisa found them so wrong that she wasn't sure if Olga believed herself what she was saying.

'Women never did anything serious in science,' Olga would say. 'It's impossible to compare their contribution. It's a God's sign, what else? If you can't do it, don't.'

'Why impossible? Why didn't?' Lisa would say. 'In some areas they did a lot. What about psychology?'

'What about it?'

Olga was a practical person, in all she did. Reading foreign journals – mostly in English, of course, - in the main public library of the country, still called Leninka then, which has been the main intellectual pleasure to Lisa for a long time (until they emigrated and the journals had become accessible to her everyday – just stretch an arm) – reading them was, it seemed, completely unfamiliar and unnecessary activity to Olga. Could it be that she's never sat like this, stooped over a foreign scientific journal in Leninka?

'What do you mean, they didn't? Women?' Lisa felt offended. 'Take Rosch, for example. It's such a powerful idea. About prototypes. And everybody picked it up, because she's a genius. And a woman.'

'Prototypes... well...' Olga clearly didn't want to argue about counterexamples.

'In fact,' Lisa added, 'prototypes have a lot to do with this discussion. And everything else, too. You know, there are prototypical birds. And they have some prototypical features. These features are more like expectations that people have about a normal bird. They fly, build nests in trees, lay eggs, they eat, most likely, I don't know, insects? But all of it is not absolutely necessary: there are chickens and ostriches. They don't fly, don't live in trees. But they are, you know, not really birds. Not quite normal birds, not what birds are likely to be, according to what we know about them from all the previous life. What we know and think is likely to be true, is a prototype. A prototype image: fly, live in a tree, eggs and insects for food. Women are like this, too,' Lisa concluded.

'Like this, why? Fly?' Olga asked.

'No, they build nests. I mean, seriously, in all cases there is something like a core of a class. By the way, they are called natural classes. All expectations are true for those members of a class that belong to the core. And there are marginal members. For them everything can be untrue. Freaks. Maybe, they are the most interesting ones.'

'Freaks are never interesting,' Olga said, 'or rather freakish behaviour.'

'Why not? Somebody like Rosch, I think, is like an ostrich among women. No expectations true. Do you know, by the way, which bird was found to be the most prototypical one, if I remember correctly?'

'Which?'

'A robin. Malinovka. Or some such.'

'You know,' Olga lingered for a moment, looking for arguments. ' Maybe, it's a beautiful theory, but you shouldn't take it literally. Women aren't like birds.'

'In what sense?' Lisa asked.

'Because birds have their own features. Most of them natural. You can't change them. You can't teach a chicken to fly. Or run like an ostrich. Women are different in this sense. I mean, they are a product of their upbringing, and the environment too, and all that stuff. If they weren't allowed, let's say, to have a tertiary education up to now, there would be no Rosch.'

'And you'd like it this way? Why? Maybe, if there wouldn't be her, there would be somebody else? Instead?'

'Who?'

'A robin among women. Or an anti-robin, depending on how you understand what a prototype is. Or an ideal. Do you think, by the way, they are the same thing, a prototype and an ideal?'

'Why shouldn't they be?'

'A prototype is where things are at, what's normal in people's mind, objectively speaking. An ideal is somebody's idea of what it should be like. What's beautiful and good.'

6.

Lisa's main responsibility at work was compiling dictionary definitions: she was part of a group of three or four who were supposed to be preparing something like a concise Russian dictionary for publication. Words she had to work on came in groups, too. Apart from other things, she had birds and documents.

'What's the difference between a petition and a request?' Lisa would ask, from her computer.

'A request is not a document. It doesn't have to be written at all. Can be oral. A petition, obviously, is a collective thing. Signed by many. Although I doubt, actually, it's a document either. It's an official appeal.'

'What's an official appeal?'

'I don't know. But there is such a thing.'

'How about...' Lisa was unsure what question to choose to make it more difficult. In fact, she was trying to see how much more she understands. It wasn't that obvious at all.

'How about... a landscape and a view?'

'Does a petition remind you of a landscape? I don't know.'

'A 'landscape' is something real and physical, The Earth's surface, and a view is something you see.'

'What about the word 'sight', then?'

One can say 'a beautiful view', but if it's not, it's rather a 'sight': one says 'what a sad sight'. Which is the reason why we say 'a room with a view', but not 'a room with a sight'.

'But what about 'sightseers'? They look for beautiful scenery, but it's derived from 'sight'.

'I don't know. 'Scenery' is another word. Nevertheless I think it's a 'view' rather than a 'sight' that implies it's pleasant to look at.'

7.

Shefinia was, Lisa thought, maybe jealous of her new involvement with words; she believed, encouraging as ever, that Lisa has moved on a lot during a few months she was doing it. To check how much she indeed has improved, Shefinia offered her an old problem: what's in common between 'youthful appearance' and 'seeing double'? Surprisingly for both of them, Lisa struck on the right answer at once: it's a semantic element 'to seem', as opposed to 'really be'.

Getting along with people in her group was a bit more difficult. There were three or four girls, including Lisa, all of approximately the same age: late twenties to early thirties. Irene seemed like an unpleasant presence, to Lisa, from the beginning: her mother taught the communist party history somewhere and in Lisa's book this meant that Irene was a person unlikely to possess the important qualities in required amounts. Which ones, Lisa was not that sure: honesty, perhaps, or what's called in English integrity. Her style was clearly different. Apart from working in the institute, she taught English somewhere, not very far from where they all sat and supposedly worked on definitions. At times Irene would tell the other girls stories of her other life, and everybody felt a bit envious, but none of them was as quick-minded in making necessary choices careerwise. And certainly not Lisa: besides, she's never had a mother who'd teach the communist party history, and this explained everything, seriously speaking.

Of all the girls, Lisa liked Fatima most. She was almost normal, by Lisa's standards. Her mother didn't teach the communist party history either, but her father was a kind of important figure somewhere in a similar Nii. Despite this, the way she talked sounded all right to Lisa. Acceptable, or almost. The thing was, maybe, not the talk, but something else. The attitude. The life style. Her lack of career aspirations and a kind of charming disorderliness and insouciance were more acceptable and closer to Lisa's heart, than anything else. The common ground was, mostly, what they call 'byt' and what famously has no equivalent in any other language but Russian: everyday difficulties with food, childcare and transport. Babysitting fees. Other ways to solve the problem.

Fatima found a privately operated kindergarten somewhere – a rarity then – and enrolled her child. Also food: she was a wonderful cook, in everybody's opinion. And there was something else: she wasn't interested in scholarly matters related to what they were, presumably, paid for, but painted little pictures with oils. With her fingers instead of brushes, for some reason, and for sale. She also had an affair – it all unfolded before their eyes, in the course of a few weeks – near, if not in, the flat of her oil pictures' dealer. To Lisa's taste, he sounded rather suspicious.

Olga knew all about the events, perhaps, even more, than all the other girls. She spoke about it like this: Fatima was hanging out at his institute for a few months, just to fuck him. Lisa had a strangely literal image of Olga's words in her head: Fatima dressed in a black frock, with her long dark hair untied hanging from a ceiling – hung not by the neck, perhaps – but how? The image became blurred there. While she was hanging out, the angry husband would call her, Olga, and ask for some information. Demand answers to his questions. Why call her, somebody please tell.

'What does he do?' Lisa asked, but didn't catch Olga's answer. The story of Fatima's adventures rolled and rumbled, fuelled by Olga's – what was it? – Lisa was unsure. The girls were listening and nodding, interested, of course. Lisa tried to visualize everything in detail: especially the beginning, to hang out to fuck. It wasn't quite clear to her, she realized, what actions and states this process would include – it was a process, wasn't it? But it was obvious that she'd rather not have a story like this told about her. This was a part that didn't need a clarification.

Vassily Ivanovich Zheltoukhov, his last name derived from what is, in Russian, 'yellow ears', was the person in charge of their 'sector, as they called it then: three girls in Olga's group, Olga herself, and another small group. He was, perhaps, the most typically Soviet boss in Lisa's short working life. Olga said so, and Lisa agreed. Before Zheltoukhov became the head of two groups in the establishment where Lisa was working now, he was, she was told, a komsomol youth leader, then a secretary of the komsomol organization at the institute, which was a step forward from a teacher's training program, in which he was enrolled having come to Moscow from somewhere – she wasn't sure where from – Belarus, maybe? He was over forty now: a slightly overweight man with a little bald spot on the top of his head, and a short dissident-ish beard, grown recently. The beard was grown to acknowledge that tempora, as well as mores, have changed. Now, during perestroika, it was no longer seen as an inappropriate escapism. Lisa has always thought that his eyes were crossed from permanent lying.

He tried not to have too many conversations with them girls, just reminded them regularly that apart from two office days, mandatory for everybody, when they all had to attend, there is also a third one, different for each one of them. And you shouldn't miss it, darlings, without a sufficient reason. Not turning up at work at all, or being absent from your workplace for more than three hours in a row, was considered as 'missing a day', Lisa has found.

Sometimes Zheltoukhov would discuss work with her. He'd call up each one of them into his tiny room next to the one where three or four girls, depending on a day, worked at the computers. The thing to discuss was, of course, dictionary definitions. They could, actually, compile or simply copy them from somewhere – any other monolingual dictionary – and maybe Zheltoukhov would prefer this – it would be simpler, no need to discuss and think so much. And the project wasn't his, after all – it was Olga's – so what's the hell? But Lisa wrote the definitions of her words herself, although she looked, of course, at times at other sources. It wasn't, after all, a school test, and besides, what did she fight for? Certainly not to copy a printed text from a book onto a white sheet of paper? This could be a way to get herself into less trouble and to keep a modest salary paid as regularly as could be at these troubled times, but, somehow, it was below her.

'A queue. Ochered',', Zheltoukhov would read. How do you spell it? Are you sure you're right?'

'Yes,' Lisa whispered. 'I am.'

'A queue,' he read on, 'is a group of people waiting for something together, usually standing in such a way that they form a line, each person following the other.' He sighed. 'Illustrations: a living queue, 'zhivaia ochered.'

'Yes,' Lisa said, 'it's a useful idiom, I think.'

'A living queue as opposed to what? Unliving? It's unclear, especially to the reader who may not be familiar with our, what d'you call it? Reality?'

'It's an interesting detail,' Lisa said, again. 'A living queue is people all standing together. As opposed to, say, a queue to get an apartment...or something else... a promotion...'

'Pardon me?'

'It's different. They don't all stand together. That's why it's not called a living queue. Just a queue.'

Zheltoukhov sighed again.

'The queue, ochered', is derived from the Old Russian word for turn, chered,' he said. 'It's not clear from what you say, although it should be.'

'I see. I'm going to add it,' Lisa said. 'But should we always say something on etymology? On other words too? I haven't been told so, so far.'

Most of what he said was true, or could be, usually, but Lisa still believed he was a fool. A fool or not, she's always felt it was unpleasant just to be next to him. It could be boring, because she was convinced, apriori, that he can never say nor do anything interesting. But she was afraid of him, so it's never been boring. Besides, when he spoke to one of them, his employees, he'd often pat their back or shoulders, perhaps, to indicate his spiritual encouragement. His wife, a middle-aged lady of very strict rules and a similar appearance, worked in another division of the same institute. Zheltoukhov would often say – Lisa heard it, at least, twice, - that he feels nausea looking at all the reference books his wife uses in her work. Lisa, felt nausea because of his habit to hug and pat his interlocutor as a sign of mental encouragement.

If she happened to remember him later, it's always made her think of two things. The first one was that she felt so much nausea then, mostly, because he was so alien to her, socially. If it wasn't so, she'd be less disgusted, and maybe even the whole story of her being a Samuel Johnson would turn out differently? Although of course, this was unlikely, and no reason to believe this much.

The other thing was how blissfully free was the country where it all had happened of the widely-spread idea that this kind of thing is abuse.

8.

After the meeting Lisa didn't like the institute anymore. The change came quickly, although, maybe, not in one day. It wasn't just that she couldn't accept the fact that Zheltoukhov was, as Olga said, a Soviet official and not at all a scholar. They all were like this. He's been promoted to where he was now by the communist party or, initially, by the komsomol, not a great deal of difference. Above him there must be, perhaps, somebody like this, too. In fact, Lisa wasn't sure who he depended on and how much of his behaviour came from the inside, and how much was caused by the circumstances and his own not quite independent situation. It's normal, she told herself again, it's everywhere. But something was abnormal. She didn't feel anymore she was incredibly lucky to be there: the meaning of it all has been lost.

Prices rose daily, they just 'let them go' and they became 'market' prices, but the salary, if it was paid at all, could feed her for a couple of days. Nothing could be done about it, apparently, apart from significantly reducing the number of people for whom the available money was divided, now ridiculously small. The meeting, was the first stage of the process devised to get rid of unwanted people, to reduce the number of those who had to be paid. Get rid of mostly new ones, who haven't 'settled properly' yet.

A month or two after 'letting go of the prices', Lisa was meeting her grandfather after work. Normally he'd take her to a restaurant, most often 'Moskva', but today they just walked the streets. Lisa was complaining.

'You see,' she said, 'I'm a very academic person, by nature. I can't, maybe, do anything else, but I start thinking of something of this kind just because I am who I am. It's natural for me, I don't know why, because of my genes or upbringing, and I dwell forever on all of it.'

'Natural?' grandfather said, 'how?'

'I don't know, I said. It may be the way I was brought up, or education. Taught to believe the main thing that matters is doing something totally irrelevant to other people, like research. Anyway, I don't know anything else. But I love to sit in the library stooped over a book or a journal and then, you know, to fantasize on my own about it. It's a full work cycle in humanities, by the way. Some people also do all kinds of surveys or experiments, to make it less of a subjective speculation, and more like a real kind of knowledge.'

'In what way more real?'

'You know, based on something other people said, or think. Tangible or measurable. But it's very time- and effort-consuming, and somehow I always end up without it. Many people do, too. Just pure introspection. But apparently it's not at all what's needed.'

'What's needed, Lisochka?'

'It depends, I think. What's needed to be left in peace to do what you've always done, I don't know, that's the point. Maybe it's because I'm not one of them. You know, haven't been with them for generations. My parents aren't in humanities, they're scientists. They have other rules. I just don't know them.'

'What rules?'

'I don't know, that the point. But they are not the same, not ours, I mean. To me, it's like much more is allowed, of what a proper technical intelligentsia person would never do, in this brilliant world.'

'For example?'

'I don't know.' Lisa thought a minute. 'Elimination... not elimination, maybe, but restructuring for unclear, that is, ideological reasons. But ideology is dead. No more.'

'It doesn't matter where you come from,' grandfather said, 'if you work well. And if you're able, of course. There were similar campaigns everywhere. You must have heard. Pseudoscience in this and that. There were quite a few. But you mustn't despair. When I first came to the city, I didn't have a high school certificate. In six months I graduated from a special 'speeded' program, passed all my tests and entered university. I've become a construction engineer, worked in aviation, you know.'

'Maybe,' Lisa had a sudden thought, 'it's all because I'm not Russian? Not quite, I mean. Accordingly, I have an imperfect relationship with the Russian language. Don't laugh. I think it sometimes, when I watch my boss. He is, I don't know, of a peasant origin. To me he sounds like his parents ploughed their land manually, without a tractor. With their own hands, I mean.'

'Don't,' grandfather seemed shocked. 'Not Russian, what could you mean? Who, then? Russian is your mother tongue, that's important. What else can be said here?'

'But you were called a cosmopolite, right?'

'It was so long ago.'

'Doesn't matter when. Something has stayed, for sure. Zheltoukhov always calls me Moiseevna. The patronymic he's invented for me. Lisa Moiseevna. 'Lisa Moiseevna, have you been to the bakery? What the prices are like?' I don't know, maybe he's afraid to go and see for himself. He's become so nervous. But it's not the point. He keeps forgetting my name, as if he's hinting at something.'

'What?'

'I don't know,' Lisa prolonged 'ow', almost whistled. Nationality, obviously, what else. Then it means something? At least, to him?'

'Cosmopolites were a mistake, Lisochka. They happen. But this one's happened only once in the course of history and is not going to be repeated. It's an accident. They happen.'

'An accident, you say. But you got fired. By the way,' she suddenly decided to show off and share her beautiful new finding, 'do you know who used this word in the negative sense first?'

'Which word?'

'Cosmopolite. I mean, who first used it negatively in Russian?'

''It's a foreign word, certainly. In the negative sense, you say? After the second World War, probably.'

'Much earlier, that's the point and the beauty. There was a journalist, before the first World War, a certain Dmitry Filosofov. He was very interested in painting and also in religion. He was writing for Mir Iskusstva, it's a kind of arty journal, very famous. Have you heard of it?'

'No'.

'I've found an interesting thing. It was Filosofov who first used 'cosmopolite' as a negative word, back then, when he argued about the religious painting with another famous person. Benoit was his name and he was a painter and also an art historian. Filosofov accused him of being a cosmopolite and said he didn't understand the importance of the Russian spirit in religious painting. Even the wording is a bit like the thirties: he said 'rootless cosmopolite'. Curious, ah?'

'But it wasn't in the thirties. The end of the forties and the early fifties,' grandfather said.

'Anyway.'

Lisa couldn't say, looking at his face, if he appreciated her finding. In the middle of Gogolevsky boulevard they entered a coffee shop, and ate, after a bit of hesitation. Then walked back to where they met. Grandfather took a train home, and Lisa, too, but another one.

9.

Ed was rereading what he's written and trying to decide: what was it? In terms of the plot and composition? What was his plan, if any? A story... a novel...about... life in Soviet academic Niis? And life in general. They are connected, obviously. A good writer would, of course, put one thing in the context of another. Everybody does it, this way or that. Ed wasn't sure, however, that he's succeeded at it.

'Yes, life in academia, or rather, life and academia,' he said, almost sang to himself, without sounding out the words. What life? Russian? What would be a good way to sum it up, then? In his novel... he realized that what he had before him wasn't a novel, not yet, anyway. In his story or...better, in his work the author is tackling or, maybe, trying to address?....the following questions: what is the reason, the prerequisite and the necessary and sufficient condition of the success in this environment? And vice versa, what can trigger a failure? 'I should add,' he thought, 'the necessary and sufficient condition of a success and failure for female junior researchers, aged twenty something. But somehow it sounds not quite all right, almost comical. I wonder why? Maybe, because the presupposition here is that there are reasons specific for this particular group, different from what they are for everybody else? Is this wrong? And if it is, indeed, wrong, not at all rooted in reality, why does it sound funny? Can it be precisely because the assumption is wrong: there is nothing peculiar about what it works like, that is success and failure, for this group? Just like anybody else. Difficult stuff,' he decided and thought he'd proceed anyway.

He realized, suddenly, that if he wants to describe everything 'as it is', he will have to describe Australia too. To deal with the question of what are the reasons of success and failure there. Are they the same? Can it be at all? And if not, what's the difference? 'It's unlikely,' he thought, 'that anybody who he could still depend on could like him afterwards. Or be inclined to help. Maybe he shouldn't write about this?'

At a certain point in time, he remembered, he believed that things like this are very similar everywhere, if not the same. They can't be the same because, obviously, the way this ladder is structured, and is supposed to be overcome, are different everywhere, but some situations tend to repeat themselves. He was sure of it, but if somebody asked, what situations, wouldn't give too many examples. One thing that kept coming up was that if, say, a dissertation was failed in Russia because of a person's unsuitable name, it could easily happen somewhere else, although it didn't have to be for the same reason, maybe even unknown or irrelevant to them. Just happen. He supposed, the logic was something like this: if it's not good enough for you, doesn't matter why, how could it be good enough for us? The idea itself is almost offensive. Or maybe the logic was different, who knows and who could ever prove it?

'I'm not up to classifying all possible situations in this field... and how they repeat themselves,' Ed thought. 'I'm not up to it, really, I don't have enough experience. But who has it, anyway, in sufficient quantities to understand well enough here and there and all kinds of places?' Doesn't matter, he did have time to observe something, no denying it.

10.

On the same day in the evening, Lisa decided to complain to her father. To hear what he'd say. She said that doesn't like the institute anymore, can hardly stand it, in fact, and maybe will soon leave.

'Where?' her father said.

'Nowhere. I will be just tutoring something, doesn't matter what, from home. Everybody knows it pays, and much better. And it makes you independent, by the way.'

'You can't take seriously this possibility.'

'Why not?'

'Well.. . I don't know...' he seemed unsure. 'I've always thought that enterprises like this are too shaky, adventurous.'

11.

Ed reread what he's written once more and noticed that there was nothing on the meeting at the institute. The one where their work was discussed and the fate decided. He skipped it, and didn't notice.

'Bad,' he thought, 'I should add it.' But he remembered surprisingly little. They discussed their work, of course. The girls'. And Lisa's too. Documents. Birds. Zheltoukhov flicked through hand-written pages: passport, certificate, application, receipt, bank cheque. There must have been something else.

'What's the difference between a document and an official letter?' he asked, suddenly. 'Look what you have here. A passport is a document confirming someone's identity. An application, on the other hand, is an official letter expressing an applicant's wish to reach a certain objective: to become an employee, to get a loan, etc. Can you say that a passport is an official letter? No? Or an application – a document? If this is so, a letter, an official one, at least, is simply a kind of document. Is it true?'

Lisa was looking for an answer, but couldn't find any. A letter is addressed to somebody, not a passport, isn't it obvious? On the other hand, what is and isn't seen as a document is almost a legal matter. How would she know? She thought that Zheltoukhov was no fool, she could see it clearly now, but what makes him so unpleasant? Maybe it's because he doesn't like her? She got it all almost for free, no effort. Compared to him, a boy from a provincial little town, or was it a village? But he didn't have to change all his papers for another name, an acceptable one, as Lisa's parents did, to make it easier for her. They thought about it just a few months before the university entry tests and started all the fuss with the paperwork. They even divorced, to make it possible, and then married again. But compared to what he's been through, maybe it's nothing. Lisa tried to imagine what it was, but she couldn't, actually. There must have been difficulties. This is why he doesn't like her. This could be enough reason in itself, but she was feeling it's not all.

'There is such a thing,' she thought, 'as a typical appearance. The way somebody's looking and what it reminds you of. It matters to me. Zheltoukhov has a typical 'Soviet boss' appearance. But if somebody asked me what it is, actually, it's hard to say. His eyes, maybe, the outline of his nose: there is something almost blunt about it. And even the beard he's grown doesn't help at all.'

Zheltoukhov felt, perhaps, that she was thinking outside the square.

'Have you reread it all yourself, Lisa?' he asked. 'By the way, should one say 'reread' or 'been rereading'?

'Both.'

The girls sat near the only window in the room, all together in a row. Besides them and Zheltoukhov there was one more person in the room, invited to attend the meeting. Petr was working at the same institute, but at least half a year spent overseas, lecturing somewhere. Lisa didn't know where, because somehow she wasn't interested. Maybe Spain, or Denmark, or Norway. Or all three places in turn, depending on a year and season. The travel was paid for by the institute. The new era was not like the previous one. One could truly say it was completely vegetarian, not in the least as blood-thirsty as before: Petr who just turned thirty didn't have to be a party member, nor anything of this kind, to travel and work overseas. Only think – he was endowed with a first-class intellect, in everybody's opinion - and say what he's thinking.

Although it seemed unexpected – suddenly Lisa decided that it was really unexpected – she knew him well enough. They saw each other regularly at all kinds of seminars for young and not so young researchers. Now he looked a bit indecisive and discouraged, as if he was trying to decide something for himself, but couldn't. Lisa was meeting his gaze now and then, and felt like she was drowning in something, like a pot of dark honey, - probably of the buckwheat kind. She was also trying to decide, if it could be that Petr likes her enough to put more importance on it than half a year of hard currency salary mattered to him. And of course, more than the institute itself mattered, which was no more than a prop, a step of a rope ladder to be folded when you don't need it anymore, she thought, maybe for the first time then. And surprised herself. But maybe, just maybe, he could pay for the tickets himself – she tried to calculate it quickly – but the official status, it mattered too – but he is affiliated with something else, she knew – so it's not all that bad. Despite all common sense which told her the opposite, she hoped that yes he did like her more than all these things – which if you think of it – he could provide for himself without the institute – although who did, really? She didn't pay much attention to what was said. They spoke well and it all seemed relevant, but the faces themselves said more to her.

'Look what you have here,' Petr said. The sound of his voice reached Lisa somewhat changed through the noise in her ears.

'Look what you have here,' he was reading her written sheets, one after another. "A sick leave certificate is a document confirming that someone's absence is due to a sickness", and so on. My question is about the illustration part. It says a sick leave certificate is issued by your local doctor for three days at once and, if necessary, is extended for more. I think it's too much of encyclopaedic information. Not really semantic in nature. You don't need to stuff the text with it so much.'

Listening to what he was saying, Lisa remembered how once they caught the same train after some kind of seminar. There were two or three stops before the Revolution Square where they both had to change trains, and they talked of everything at once, like work, and money, and babysitting which was always on Lisa's mind then.

'It's all going tip-top, we're a highly organized mob,' Lisa said. 'I'm home once a week, on my free day, my mum once too, and my mother-in-law as well.'

'It makes just three days, what about the other two?'

'One of them, didn't I say? – takes my husband, and the other one isn't a problem, we share it: I go to work in the morning, and when I come back around midday, he can leave. Until late, if he wants to. It makes, basically, a full day.'

Lisa was filled with satisfaction and pleasure of solving an unsolvable, if everybody wasn't there to do their share, problem. And felt really strange when she met a cold stare: he dealt with all these matters in a different way, or rather they dealt with themselves without him, although there were a few children, she knew.

'There was something else, too, relevant.' She made an effort to remember. 'They spoke about the verb 'to miss'. Its valencies. He wanted to see, if she could name them. Who missed something, what was missed and what with. Petr missed a target shooting. Or shooting with a gun. That's why one can miss it with a bullet or with a gun, but hardly both: he missed a target with a bullet with a gun. But it may be 'from': missed it with a bullet from a gun. What else can you miss it with? It's easy to miss a target with a small stone. If you throw a big stone, there is less chance of missing a target.

'Yes,' Petr said. Suddenly Lisa switched on and started listening again. 'Yes, too much of encyclopedic information is something you have everywhere, Lisa. It's not just one definition, or two. I think it's unnecessary. Why would you need so much detail?'

'Why?' Lisa finally found enough courage to say something. 'A reader may be interested. Especially a foreign one. If the dictionary is indeed aimed at foreign learners, as they told us. Has it been decided? I think it matters a lot who our reader will be, obviously. And anyway, there is a point of view that information like this is part of a word's meaning.'

Later there was talk of something else, and then again something else: she didn't listen well. Petr and Zheltoukhov discussed other people's work, sometimes let them answer. Finally, it was finished: it was around lunch time. There were no notes taken, nor any decision announced. But clearly theirs was a lost cause. Although there was nothing to compare it with, at least not in her experience, it seemed decided.

As it often happened, Petr caught the same train as Lisa at the station, after it all finished.

'I'm sorry I couldn't protect you,' he said. 'But your sick leave certificate entry was good.'

It was unclear when he said 'protect you', did he mean her, Lisa, or all of them as a group. And maybe it wasn't important either. Where do you hide a leaf? A tree? In a forest.

Lisa was going home by train and swayed a little, leaned back and forward, to enhance its little pushes. It was a bit like love making, she thought. Or was it, really, an anticipation of parting, a separation? Bits and pieces of the meeting she just attended were running through her head. Rewind, then fast forward. Again rewind. Where was a clue? It was scary and humiliating. Obviously, they've chosen them, her especially, as scapegoats. But why? And what for? The why part was clear: because the money they had wasn't enough to pay everybody. Then 'what for' was obvious, too: with fewer people to pay, there would be larger salaries. But there could be another 'what for': what was it they've been punished for? For being too young, maybe? Too conceited? People who've planned it all felt more sorry for people who have been there for a while? Maybe even depended on them in some way? And didn't like her being so sure. Having a certain kind of appearance and being a type. Whatever she was a type of, Zheltoukhov must have found it unpleasant. Like he himself was appalling to Lisa.

Her thought turned back to Petr and she tried to remember, when she liked him most. What did he say then? 'When are you going to give us a talk and make us all happy?' Yes, quite like this. 'Make us happy'. She liked it. And also that he went around the table to ask it. 'I don't know,' Lisa said. 'Maybe, a few weeks. I'm getting ready.' She touched her ponytail above her neck and thought that it's time to wash her hair. Instead of it today she washed the floor, hurriedly, before the nanny would arrive. She was a woman of strict rules and could start a scene or even leave, if she found it wasn't sufficiently clean everywhere. 'Yes, in a few weeks,' Lisa said. 'I haven't decided yet, how to formulate my topic.'

Then the times changed almost suddenly, and everything else too. The old wisdom so many lived by that a hundred rubles is enough for everything, and maybe even more than enough, because there is nothing to buy anyway and who'd like to queue for hours – simply wasn't true anymore. It wasn't enough, but not enough meant different things in each case. Approximately at this time Petr started teaching both in Moscow and overseas. He also found a new area of interest: the language of social and political discourse. Before perestroika, it was a forbidden subject, if not altogether unthinkable, but now it was allowed. Lisa found his analysis of newspapers, Soviet history textbooks and the like, lacked real content.

Somehow it was all too shapeless, too conformist to her. What's so interesting about saying that one had to read all the Soviet history books and newspapers between the lines – saying it now, when it's one of the most popular topics for journals and newspapers themselves, and is not in the least frowned at? And also don't you have to read all the new ones, textbooks and other stuff, that is, between the lines? In a different sense? How it is different, she thought, would be really interesting to know, but it wasn't about it. Yes, it lacked real content. And she even shared her opinion with somebody then. Was this the reason? Offended pride? She couldn't understand how one can be so proud, but she knew that one could. He paid her back for everything: her insufficient praise for his achievements – didn't she say the analysis wasn't specific enough and meaningless, in fact – and also her indifference to his charm. What, she wondered, was more important? The most offensive thing?

And there was the question of money, too. It came up when they once talked about how much one's salary will increase after a 'zashchita', a PhD. Somebody asked her – not Petr, somebody older, who she hardly knew at all, – asked her why not get it all done sooner, if her work is, in fact, nearly ready. Why wait? And the money will increase.

'Yes, by twenty five rubles,' Lisa said. 'Not enough to pay a babysitter for a week. And I'm going to be without an extra summer leave, that all distance students get, from then on. No.'

She said it then because she was in the habit of always saying what she thought. She could see now that it would be better, perhaps, not to. What Petr did then struck her. He seemed indignant, almost angry, as if what he himself was thinking of twenty five rubles was different. 'It's his wife who earns there,' Lisa thought. 'Lessons or something like it.' Apparently, it was this thought, along with other things, that hasn't been forgiven.

Ed reread his written pages and felt he's tired. Procrastinating. If he's going to follow the chronology, he'll have soon to describe what happened later. The first trip overseas, the return home, him being fired, them departing to Australia, him getting a scholarship, emigration, two long trips back home. This should be his time frame, if he wants to tell it all. But he felt he didn't. There were too many details he didn't want to resuscitate, articulate and contemplate. A lot of things. But he had to, if he wants to deal with this task he's assigned himself: to tell about the way success and, maybe more importantly, failure works in the environment he's been in. The task seemed a bit like a research question. Lisa has been taught to identify and formulate them, before starting work.

But he doesn't have to follow the way it all happened, he decided, he can choose, if he wants to, anything in the middle of the time. Fragments, bits and pieces. Things he remembered better, the ones which aren't too hard to tell. And he can move along in circles, or maybe dashed lines, propelled by any connection between episodes, whatever they can be, topical or otherwise. Above the time. It appeared for some reason that one cannot move above the time in circles, but why, really? Why not?

12.

Take Petr. He came up in Lisa's life once or twice more, when she was living in Australia already. During her second or third year of scholarship she's found out that Petr translated or, rather, edited a translation of Lisa's supervisor's last book. It was a woman, by the way. (Why is it that I'm always supervised by women, Lisa wondered; except Zheltoukhov, of course – and Semen – he was, clearly, the best thing that ever happened to her in this respect –or was it because she was simply too young then and her attitude to many things hadn't taken yet the hard shape it acquired later?). A woman academic who spoke remarkably good Russian found Petr's translations terrible, after she's just looked at them. But for some reason – why Lisa could never tell – was firmly convinced that it can't be his own fault. Whose fault it was didn't matter that much, but it couldn't be his: he can't, after all, correct every word and sentence himself. This was something the supervisor academic set off to do herself. Lisa was offered a role of a native emergency help: she could be asked about really unclear cases, of which there weren't many at all, for one reason or another.

This time Lisa was, or tried to be, wise enough not to utter a word of surprise on the two eternal Russian questions of what is to be done and who is to blame. Who is to blame, if not Petr, who was in charge of it all? But it turned out that some people, Petr included, were above all suspicion. Somehow Petr's reputation by this time was such that it all simply couldn't be his fault. Nor anything else, for that matter. No little flaws, wrongly chosen words and badly formed sentences could spoil his reputation. How it's shaped – a reputation like this – Lisa has never learned. If she didn't count, of course, her observations of Petr during that long forgotten meeting. He seemed so unsure of what to do then – was it some kind of a fork in the road to him? How much this and similar incidents – there could be more, she thought – actually helped his reputation, she didn't know. But clearly it was a universal asset, a currency converted without loss, and a power stretchable as far as Australia. And small insignificant things like ugly under-edited texts can't really influence what's happening to a reputation like this.

And there was something else, she remembered. She offered her help more times than it was needed, or welcome. And couldn't hide, in the end, her limited respect for Petr's achievements. But maybe, again, it wasn't this that was important. To Lisa he was a mystery, a living embodiment of that question about what success in this world could be conditioned by. Not very well educated, in terms of languages, she thought – he spoke only three main European ones, and all three not too well, and not very intelligent either – when was the last time she heard something interesting or new from him? They even argued, once, about how new a new idea in this field should be and what it actually means. He was none of these things – so what was the secret of his power over people? Maybe, the manner of speaking itself? Authoritative and very persuasive from his early days, never rude and combative, but acceptable to all those he depended upon, and at the same time not quite repulsive to those who had nothing to do with Soviet and post-Soviet officials, reasonably refined. A gold section of everything. Or, maybe, it was not so much what was said as the sound of his voice, undoubtedly beautiful? But damn it, he wasn't an actor, was he?

The last time Lisa heard of Petr in Australia was in connection with a strange discussion: it was about managers. If they are needed. Apparently, nobody ever said that they could be not, but still there was a discussion in those few Russian journals she could reach, in which some influential people participated, Petr included. She found it on the net: he argued that managers have something to do with stability and some other good things, which ones she's immediately forgotten. Said something which had nothing to do with his profession, not directly, anyway, but still reflected – what was it? – perhaps the perception of life in general. It's the logic of life – Lisa realized – that we feel about it differently, whatever one can believe in, consciously. And realized one more thing, immediately after: he is a kind of manager himself. Manager of science. Was getting there all his life, and now it's happened, obviously.

13.

Ed sighed. It's about time he'd finish. All this has already touched on the Australian period of his life, although he was not going to do it. They say you mustn't spit in your own food, and other things like this. It must be true. The only thing is, if you follow this kind of logic, you must never sing anything but praise to all sources which have anything to do with what you are. Which is, basically, everything around you.

They are strange doubts, he thought, who'd have them now? Some people believe that commonsense and the ethics meet each other at a certain point. The sad thing is that he keeps missing this point – what with, what from? But it doesn't matter, if you think about it well enough. What really matters is that there is such a point – or, maybe, it doesn't matter either?

If you look at the end result – which of course, justifies the means of its achievement – who'd ever doubt it – Petr was doing everything right and Lisa was wrong. The question of what she'd done wrong was always on Lisa's mind, and the answer was, although always different, hard to digest. She wasn't sure enough of herself, and maybe something else, to correct them. Mistakes. Or was it something else she lacked? The practical sense? The common sense? Are they the same thing, by the way? Both senses, the practical and the common one were replaced by something else in her. Charm?

Yes, mistakes. Lisa thought they'd made a mistake when emigrated. But everybody did it then, if not before. The 1992 to her, like most other people, was the year when market prices have been introduced. Empty shelves and desperate walking of streets in search of a little bit of food was replaced with something completely new and unfamiliar. Theoretically beautiful and right because everybody she knew was, of course, pro freedom. But not always tolerable in real life, at least, not then, in the beginning. Later, Lisa thought, everything has changed for the best. Immeasurably. But why immeasurably? Most of these changes could be measured in terms of the level of inflation, typical consumption and something else like it.

Immeasurably changed for the best, Lisa thought, coming to visit from her far-away new-found home. Back then they've made a decision that took the least effort, probably. And somehow reminded her of an old joke: do you like cheese? Yes, of course, but not enough to eat it. Do you like freedom and market prices? They did, but not enough to eat it. And the answer seemed simple: don't eat it, just go. Simple and so many times tried before us. The only difference was, Lisa thought, the only, but not a small one, that this solution was not often chosen and used in such a terrible hurry. It looked like there was no time to think: everybody kept saying that nobody knows what we're going to eat next winter. Everybody, however, was eating something. But the worst thing was, probably, that it wasn't a fear of famine that made them go and pack so fast. Not that, but just being offended by your own boss. Which is quite a different matter, although the two could be related, of course. Lisa could never get along with bosses, or almost never .There was something in her that made it impossible. It must be, she thought, what one calls an inner independence. Although what kind of independence there could be in a girl? Is independence a hate of teamwork? But she didn't have that, she was sure. What's so strange then in being chosen as one of those made redundant people, when the money they had at their disposal had become clearly not enough for everybody? If the reason was her own qualities, the explanation would be different. But the whole Olga's group had to go, and although it obviously was done to save money, Zheltoukhov was happy to get rid of a rival at his own level. Or the next level below, and threatening to move up to his. Both these things could matter, couldn't they. But it wouldn't be so sudden and impacting people like her, if it wasn't for the time.

And soon she was transported into something completely new, unthinkable before then. Everything was it, including what she had to do: she was packing and wrapping the first chapter of her dissertation, most of it written in Moscow, in stiff and inflexible English sentences. Homesickness became indistinguishable to her from a frustration with the alien grammar. An alien sense of good and bad and beautiful. Which is just one step away from being simply tired of choosing a suitable sentence structure. A structure that would combine it all in an acceptable way: a subject – a predicate – an object. Or: a subject – a predicate – a recipient. If the recipient isn't Zheltoukhov, then who? Where could she find a suitable one?

14.

Ed stopped to think. It looked like he said it all before. And Lisa seemed, somehow, too simple in this. Unbelievable. 'Does she look alive?' he thought. 'Or, is there a level of complexity somewhere that you simply can't go beyond? Once you've crossed it, nobody is going to believe in your character. A heroine. It's even worse, if the maximum allowed complexity is different for everybody, but how else can it be? Same? He reread a few pages and decided that he's chosen the right voice for her: women speak like this, and even write like this: as if they were speaking. And always have a convincing heroine in their books. To see everything through their eyes. If Lisa was suitable for this, he hasn't decided yet.

'What's missing?' he asked himself once more. 'What makes it seem simpler and cruder, than it was? Is it because the attitude, the way we see emigration is, like most things, inherited? We take it from our parents and grandparents? Her grandfather - not the one who was once fired as a cosmopolite, but the other one – moved to Israel when he was already over eighty. And died there, in less than a year. But her father, his son, had always been a Russian patriot. As well as her mother. Is it, she wondered, that we are always different, at least on the surface of it, from our parents?

The attitude to work, she thought, is something we inherit too. From her mother Lisa inherited the hate of normal 9 to 5 office life. And her love of the so-called library days. And from her father his never ceasing desire to keep digging holes in his academic garden, whatever it was he was planting in them. The holes, in her case, had to be in a different field and the rules of digging were not the same at all. But she didn't know this in the beginning.

15.

When the three and a half years were over, the question of maybe going back home came up. Lisa had, for a while, a feeling that this was actually the most important thing that happened over these years. The two trips home - she couldn't manage more. Later this vision has drifted away from her somewhere, became fuzzy and blurred. Many things happened between the time when they moved to that small capital city where she was paid her scholarship money and the second trip to Moscow. The last unsuccessful attempt to go back.

The thing Lisa remembered most of her first time in Canberra was the bus. She traveled by bus, daily. And it took her a while to learn where to get off. Or was it the view she found striking? She'd catch a bus and look outside through an incredibly clear window, as clear as the cool air behind it, bright and shiny, all of it unbelievably soaked with sun. For some reason, she could never understand why, she'd always feel sad and miserable looking outside the window through this light-filled air. Everything seemed strangely coloured, as if it was painted, like white roses painted red in Alice's Wonderland. Or as if she looked at it through a plastic wrap. Lisa was trying to peel off this imaginary membrane, with a stare, and sometimes she did.

Most of the time she felt frightened, although there was nothing to be frightened of. The autumn leaves were red and yellow, the air crisp, and the sun bright all year round. There is a fountain the bus passed by, and a merry-go-round. Enjoy. Summer was now winter, and vice versa. The yearly cycle had stumbled for a moment, and then made a step forward and ran. Not that it mattered: she never was dependent on weather that much. But the fear has become a background to everything, a constant habit. Although things she was afraid of, were, probably, she thought now, all the wrong ones. Spiders, for instance. They say there are some terribly dangerous ones here. And once she almost flooded the house, trying to get one off the ceiling in the living room, with a stream of water from a garden hose. The spider, it turned out later, wasn't dangerous. A huntsman, not poisonous at all. It wasn't that she had nobody to ask about it: they even had some local friends and acquaintances. But there was no time, she was sure: what if the spider jumps down and attacks her first?

And she was constantly worrying about the money: what if they stop paying her? She didn't know, what's supposed to happen in this case, but didn't want to try. A fear worth of a worthy conscience. She wasn't so much homesick then?

But later came a time when she started liking it all. No, this, probably, couldn't be. But why not? Everything is possible, they say. When ten years later they moved, another life has started. The new city was bigger and better, than the first, and above all, was at sea. Something she's always wanted. It came, probably, from her grandfather who used to take her to Iurmala, the Soviet pretend Europe.

The new city was like nothing she's known before, but if you start looking for something, of things she's seen it was most like Odessa. She's seen it once, at a conference. The same holiday-resort-like blissful lazy attitude was in the air and commonsense seemed to be diluted with a healthy dose of neglect for all that was reason. It could not be true at all, she knew, but she liked thinking it was. There were so many different people and at least half of them seemed not giving a damn about succeeding in any usual sense. Although, again, this could be a wrong impression: the way people look can be misleading, they say, and even if it's not, you need a skill to read appearances. Which makes it more interesting, of course.

The street life sprouted with branches and, like a river, broke into little creeks; one could simply bend down to drink from it anywhere. Like a park circus show that didn't even have to be paid for. Or endless and endlessly different cafes in little streets. There was something she especially liked about all this entourage, something encouraging, almost calming. What it was, she couldn't tell, or didn't want to. Compared to the previous place, everything wasn't so new and glassy. There was solid matter and age to things and houses, and they weren't so deadly transparent. But so free and careless. These might have been tourist thoughts, tourist impressions – but she liked them anyway.

Or, maybe, the reason was people? The old distinction between intellectual work and manual labour seemed irrelevant to them, unimportant. Who are, by the way, acrobats in this dichotomy? You never know.

Lisa got a job in a nursing home and started making collages. Before she cut and glued her paper, she treated it with wax. It was an old method invented, in fact, for cloth, somewhere near Java, in Indonesia, and she loved it the moment she read about it in an old book, found by chance in a street pile. People have known about it for a long time, but she's learned it here. She's been completely happy, for a while. Life was almost beautiful, and had as much in common with the previous one, as Soviet Java cigarettes that her parents used to smoke had with the real island. She didn't care if it was much.

16.

But there must have been something between these two points, the two trips to Moscow. The first one, five years after the move to Australia, was, for whatever reason, an unclear, blurred memory. It still seemed possible then to go where you've come from. Only superficial, alien to what you really are, things stood in the way. Like inflation, survived and tamed by everybody at this point in time. But hated by all she had to deal with. To the point of wanting to live where there was none. If she wanted to live here, however, she had to count on something. Private lessons were her only thing, an urgent financial safety measure always used by Mother, before it all fell apart. Nothing new here, at least not for her. But this was safe. And if she could do it before they went, obviously, it wouldn't be worse now, should be better.

The city felt strangely her own. And strangely, her daughter managed at school. Maybe because the teachers still couldn't see her as a stranger from nobody knows where, or because she always did. Lisa never thought much about it, again, up to a point. Until another child started school. She realized then that of all the things she's seen in Moscow during that first trip she herself resembled most a fat Georgian woman she met at school once. At a parents' meeting. All other people hated her, or so it seemed. Perhaps for her money that came nobody knows where from, or a very clear accent. 'How much time do you spend on homework, Aida Rashidovna,' the teacher asked her, if the woman was in her class herself. 'Fife,' Aida said. 'Whole fife, capisci?' That is, five hours. To become a woman like that, it doesn't take much time. Five years was more than enough.

A month had gone, and then another. Summer was finished, then autumn. They sniffed the air a bit longer and went off – it was time to rent out the flat, since nobody was living there anyway. And it would help with other things, of course.

It turned out to be impossible to go back where you've come from, after all. Not anymore.

But she made one more attempt, seven years later. Not a serious one – but just to see what she could do, if she came back. It's lasted a few months and convinced her that it could be quite good, actually. Lessons and stuff. Convince everybody else to come back with her seemed impossible.

17.

Ed reread what he's written once again and tried to see what he's missed. If his emigration itself was a mistake, what good could come from it? But why not? Until some time it seems strange, but then you realize that a victory is just being here – it's what you see before you, everywhere. A victory is a lack of failure, and a failure, a real one, is something that comes from within, it can't be done to you, forced onto you by some kind of crazy unimportant person absorbed up to his ears in paperwork. Right? Of course it is. 'It's all because,' he thought, 'we hate authorities so much. A Soviet habit of conscience. A habit of contradiction. If certain people, mostly those in power, think and say this and that, I will think the opposite. And certainly I can't depend on them. Maybe physically, but not in what I feel.'

He looked around and tried to imagine how many people in the street could share this feeling. 'An absurd thing, really, if you carry it through all the way, but it gives you strength. The only thing is you have to stop somewhere. You can't live with it here, or maybe, you can?'

An automated dissent is a good name for it. An automated dissent is wonderful, because it protects you from failure. Failure cannot be inflicted upon you by certain people, bad ones. A victory is simply an absence of failure. A victory is when you have no failure. Like when you suddenly see that you're made, mostly, from automated dissent. To see it as it is, and not to take too seriously, is something good already, good drawn from bad.

He shook his head: it may be true, but he must put a limit to it somewhere. Alice said that there should be conversations in a book, but where are they?

18.

Her new life by the sea sometimes seemed to Lisa happening to somebody else. She's changed so much! Finally, she got away from the past. Seriously! She couldn't tell why she wanted to break away from the past so much, but was sure it's necessary. Maybe because it was clear that in that former identity – 'there are quite many people out there writing on identities, whatever the word is in Russian,' she realized and felt relieved – in that former identity – there was something terribly hopeless and helpless about it? Or was the desire for change her new perspective, itself a result of a non-failure, idiosyncratically understood? But she wouldn't hesitate to tell what it was that made the previous life hopeless. There was too much of something, and something lacked, too. She was sure of what it was too much – too much of meaningless 'officization' as they call it, following somebody who's invented the clumsy word for it. All academic life, she thought, requires a kind of this wrapped into an office cocoon conscience. Maybe, its best version, but still... Or is it a non-significant, superficial similarity? And there was too little of everything else, especially the idea that there could be something else, other possibilities.

If one faces another way of life once in a lifetime, say, in army training camps, in summer, and runs from it under some kind of invented pretext, then one must miss something. Lisa was sure of it. What precisely? Maybe, even all of it? But of course, there always have been holidays outside army training camps. Mountain and boat trips. Sweet smell of carefully arranged deprivation, cooked from a concentrate, but easily digestible. And much more varied and funny than any deprivation you can't choose yourself. A noble passion for travel dressed in clothes made from the iron curtain, which was pulled down to its full length then. Nobody she knew has ever crossed the border, of course, up to a point in time. Romanticized deprivation was a way to learn more. Often the one and only.

So when Lisa found Polina's job ad in a local newspaper, she felt immediately happy.

'Call Polina,' the name was Russian, and there was a kind of promise in it, to be honest. Lisa called, and came for an interview: it was one of the inner city suburbs. Where could Polina, Lisa wondered, find the money to buy a house like this for a nursing home she owned? It was old and obviously falling apart, but the location... Polina was a rather young woman, approximately Lisa's age, with hair that used to be called 'auburn'. She spoke English to Lisa. She learned, among other things, that Polina was once a trained teacher, at some unclearly distanced times, somewhere in an unknown corner of the Soviet Union. 'French language and literature,' she said. 'I pay cash in hand,' she added. 'You'll be starting at eight and finishing at two.' She glanced at Lisa once again, measuring her up. 'Thirty dollars,' she said, this time in Russian. A fuzzy thought about how much it will be for an hour – too little, is it not? – flied through Lisa's head but never shaped into words. What's the difference? Is she hungry, or what? The important thing is, it's easy to get here. And she's in. And later she'll see.

'Your responsibilities will include,' Polina was saying. Lisa was looking aside and scanning the walls for photos and other interesting things. There was a grand-piano in the corner – who was it for? The residents who lived in the home all had early Alzheimer. A few Russians, among them. Polina obviously had a weak spot for them. Maybe because it was easier for her to get along with the relatives. Who knows what made her make a step like this – to buy a nursing home – but she was not at all indifferent to other people's opinion. And whether they liked her. Lisa looked at photos on the walls and wondered whose they might be, and if any of these – what d'you call them? residents? – remembers it. Or not at all? While Lisa was trying to work out whose picture was where – she just met them all – about three and a half dozens people with memory difficulties – Polina decided it was time to speak about life. To complain. She complained about work, of course, difficulties with finding work in her professional area. Or what was it. 'I love French,' she said, lowering her voice confidentially. 'I love children, I love working with them.' It was, Lisa suspected, a kind of ritual: complain. Complain in your language. Complain to compatriots, or otherwise...Otherwise they won't see you as a good person.

'I'd go work at school,' she said again, 'but the papers, you must know.'

'I don't know,' Lisa said. 'I'm from somewhere else, I mean, it's somewhere else I studied. Can't you translate them? Recognize?'

'It's very, very difficult,' Polina said. 'I've found out. I think it's all because of money differences. You know what's a teacher's wage in Russia is. Virtually nothing. And compare it to here.'

Lisa forced herself hard to hear all about the wage, not to switch off, and suddenly remembered how she met a French teacher at a parents' meeting in an Australian school, years ago. Lisa thought then that she made strange mistakes: in unpronounceable endings of a past tense. If they sounded alike, she believed the spellings were the same too, although it wasn't, really, so. The tense was called Imparfait. Not that Lisa was a guru in this stuff, but she still remembered a few basic facts from that long ago time when she had to learn it all to pass the university entry tests. Imparfait. It turned out later that the teacher's specialty was something else: German, maybe, or sports. But she taught other things, too.

'Tell Polina?' Lisa was unsure. 'In detail?' She told the teacher then about her mistake, couldn't help it, but no consequences, surprisingly, followed. Lisa had to make an effort not to tell it all to Polina – when complaining, she looked and sounded a bird of Lisa's feather all right - or did she mention some of it, after all? Making an effort to tell as little as possible, Lisa got up and followed Polina around the house. She opened doors and told Lisa what's where.

Trying to follow her 'step-for-step', the way they walked in the mountains on snow, tied to a rope, Lisa thought that all that she's having now is no more than a logical conclusion of her love for adventure. So have it and enjoy. Out-of-the ordinary and other things like it. 'Polina is trying to see now,' she realized, 'how hopeless my situation is.' Something must have been depending on it, but Lisa didn't quite see what. 'Money, obviously? Something else? Her attitude? If it's not hopeless enough, she won't like me? I wonder what conclusion she's come at,' Lisa thought. The more she tried to put herself into Polina's shoes, and see things from her point of view, the more she felt she couldn't.

Polina was hunting people in hopeless circumstances, this bit was clear. At least this was a sensation one got dealing with her, her aura. But otherwise she wasn't bad at all. Edible.

A new life has started. Lisa washed the floors in the morning, around eight o'clock. It seemed so early to her. It was almost dark in Peter's room, but she felt a kind of perverted pleasure, who knows what from? After the floors, she washed people. Sometimes three or four in a row.

She could see everything from below – she had to lean down a bit, following a mop in her hands – and the perspective she could see it from seemed incredible, almost unheard of to Lisa. Like Sofia Perovskaia. Although, of course, it's unlikely that she had to wash the floors...but... who knows...Or who else was it?

Narodovoltsy? That nineteenth century revolutionary group, called so after the will of people. She could see everything now from a completely different point of view. Only her own. And it doesn't matter if it's an observation point high in the mountains, on a house roof or just a little elevated bump on the road. It's all relative. What matters is to see something new. Now the point of view has gone down somewhere, and everything appeared big and strange from below. But unusual, new, and the angle, the perspective is interesting.

Looking at Peter's photo from below, at an angle which was approximately equal to that between the mop handle and the floor, Lisa was trying to decide: is this him? Well, she knew, of course, it was him, but psychologically? Should one believe he is the same person as he was then, identical to himself? Or not at all? Sometimes it looked like yes he was, and sometimes – no. Sometimes Peter would come to his senses, become his old self, almost – although, of course, how could she know what he was like – all she saw was a pale shadow – and say something. 'I want,' he said. What followed, was indiscernible, to her. You, maybe? And despite his age – he was around eighty now, Lisa thought, and frail too, - once, when she was already at the front door, ready to go home, he grabbed her by the neck and tried to pull back. It would be a passion crime, but he was too weak.

Polina organized an occupational health and safety meeting, to talk about things, this incident included. Lisa had to come from home especially for this, at an odd time outside her roster.

'I'm as uneasy as ever at meetings,' she thought. 'What have I learned, really? Some things don't change. Meetings like this, for example.'

Lisa sat at the meeting and listened to instructions on what to do if Polina's house caught fire. This seemed incredible to Lisa: why would it catch fire? If Peter won't go completely crazy, of course, and light it up? She listened to all dos and don'ts Polina listed and tried to recall other things like this. Similar in a sense. Little scenes from the past. Play, rewind, play again.

It was also some kind of meeting. How many years ago? Twelve? Ten? She was attacked then – that's what she called it to herself – 'attack' – by what was his name? she never found out. Strange, but what her name was, he seemed to know. The main tool of dressing up his thought into words for him must have been understatement, she decided. Lisa just learned then what it was - understatement. In theory, at least. She was trying to see what he meant, and include understatement in the picture. – but did she get it right? As if she looked at things through a plastic wrap. Burned and fused with other things in some places. The thing was, according to what's his name, that there were too many writers in Australia, many of them hardly literate at all. Especially Aborigines and the like. Overseas students who've come nobody knows where from, what kind of communist fantasy land. Is it not communist any more? All the worse for it, if I, whoever I may be, can't even understand what it's become now. Lisa wasn't sure that all of this could be classed as an understatement, if she knew what it was, of course. Perhaps not. But anyway, she said something in response. Trying to hide how angry she was – remember understatement! - to shield and justify. Not herself, of course, some kind of imaginary 'other'.

Later she told about this conversation to K. They didn't think the same about it. She was aggressive, he said. What you say, the content, and the vehicle, the way it's said, are not the same thing.

'Why it's me who's aggressive,' Lisa argued. 'He's started it. And he knew who I am. I have no idea who he is.'

'Not a good thing, by the way.'

'Perhaps. But why should I know? And how? But I agree, the way you say it is not that important. Not the main thing.'

'What's the main thing?'

'The main thing is,' Lisa said, 'that I shouldn't have to compete with him.'

'Why?'

'Because I'm a woman. But this is not so, especially here in Australia. I mean, to survive normally, like everybody else, you have to compete with him. But it's not the worst thing.'

'What's the worst one?'

'The worst thing, to me, is not that I have to compete. The worst thing is that the rules of this competition are different for me and for him. If you have to compete, they should be the same.'

'What d'you mean?'

'Just what's happened. What is an aggressive outburst for me, is an acceptable behaviour for him. And it's like this not only on the personal level. In writing, too. What for him would be labeled 'an angry young man' attitude, and seen as rather likeable, even if, maybe, a bit overdone, for me is hardly acceptable. Again.'

'It has to be proven.'

'I think it's obvious. I've come across it so many times. Maybe, it's starting to change now, but just starting. But it's not the only point where the rules are different.'

'Where else?'

'The worst part of it is that my personal life is everybody's business. Not just mine, any woman's, apart from, maybe, some higher-standing ones. And plenty of people think that if they don't approve of it, the personal life, that is, I don't deserve anything at all. But it doesn't apply to him. He can be anything and do anything, but everybody is ready to admit he's got his good sides and achievements, if, of course, he'll have any. And by the way, some really unpleasant things follow from it.'

'What things?'

'Like pressure to have or not to have sex. Rather to have than not. In old days people were pressed into not having it, now it's the other way round. Which is not at all better, if not worse. Because the information available is kind of ... what do you call it? There is more of it, you know.'

There was a pause.

'And overall, what's his main strength?' Lisa said.

'What?'

'There are three. The first one is that he's a man and never dealt with all those problems that can make somebody else's life a bit difficult. The second strength is that he's a native speaker of the language he lives within. And the third one is almost the same as the second one. It's a strength and a weakness at the same time.'

'That is?'

'I mean, he's had a normal calm life. Like other people with the same background. Without having to travel to another part of the world, least of all permanently. A totally predictable life. Or so it seems, from the outside. One can argue, of course, that there is no such thing as a totally predictable anything.'

'I don't know. Why should it matter?'

'Because it's the reason why he's bored with himself. It looks so to me. Nothing to say. Nothing he'd want everybody to know about, mostly, because they know it all anyway. Of course, there doesn't have to be a connection between these two things, but then you need something else.'

'Like what?'

'A gift. There is no gift there, clearly.'

Lisa listened to Polina talking about fire safety and remembered all the details of this long forgotten conversation. When did it happen by the way? She's forgotten this bit. Or suppressed.

It was at the same meeting that Lisa first met Beverly. Actually, there were two: a Beverly working in the home and another one living there. They sat together, because a possibility of fire, of course, was a matter of importance.

'Beverly...' at times Beverly number one tried to ask Beverly number two a question. For the rest of it she couldn't find words.

'Yes, Beverly?' Beverly number two was always ready to address all concerns of Beverly number one. 'Yes, I'm here.'

At times Lisa met Beverly number one alone in the house. It was Lisa's responsibility, after all, to change her bed and clothes. She always tried to tell her something.

'I'm going to hospital tomorrow,' she told her once and then repeated a week and two later. Was it just that she didn't feel alright? Heard something? But obviously she didn't go there. Lisa felt almost afraid – what of, she couldn't tell – suspected something – what precisely, hard to explain. She never knew, actually, who'd get Beverly's money in this case. And anyway, it was not her business at all.

They say there is an end to everything. Later Lisa could never remember when she first had an unexpected thought that Polina underpays her, and a lot. And she can't stand it anymore. Where and how she's found out that it shouldn't be so, she couldn't remember either. That it should be about twice as much? A bit more than twice? Somehow she did find out, perhaps she had a good ear for this kind of information. They say 'a good ear for music' or 'a good ear for languages.' By the way, there is nothing like this in Russian, only a good, or all-catching eye. She had, it turned out, a good ear for this kind of thing. Maybe this was, in fact, a sign of latent or not so latent aggression? Looking for means to fight?

This time luck was on Lisa's side. At least, at first. The first thing she did was to ask Polina for the difference between what she's paid her up to date, that is for the three months Lisa's spent with her, and what she had to, according to the rules. Polina just ignored her, and Lisa started visiting all kinds of people who'd provide her with a free consultation on what to do and act on her behalf. But the process turned out to be neither pleasant nor easy. She'd found an address in a book, took a train there and then walked endlessly, it seemed to her, along an unfamiliar street, one of the central ones, however, all the way up to an impressive skyscraper. But she didn't have to take an elevator to any floor. Instead she had to make a phone call from a large rather empty hall below and tell somebody what her problem was. She did call, but still didn't have to take an elevator up. She had to make a time and come again a few days later. And even do it more than once: most people who had to help her did it reluctantly, and it took time.

All this time she kept working at Polina's, like before: three times a week, every second day. The way Polina treated her, and Lisa responded, didn't change either. Not even a little bit: they both didn't give a damn, it seemed, what a happy feeling! Especially compared to all this meaningless suffering during her graduate years. And she didn't feel uneasy at all. Lisa decided that it will be honest and absolutely necessary to write Polina a letter and explain in it what she was going to do, and did so. Most people probably wouldn't, she suspected, and who cares what's honest when you try to get the underpaid money from your employer through court.

She wanted most to get what Polina owed her at lunch. It was called a 'lunch break'. Somehow from the name itself followed that it cannot last an hour, like most lunch breaks she encountered so far did. At first it didn't last at all: Polina believed that there is no need to dilute her six-hour shifts with breaks. But with time Lisa found out that she had a right to one and insisted. And got it. She'd run out for half an hour, around twelve – it's been about four hours after her eight o'clock start time – and breathed in, almost swallowed sunny air, beautifully adorned shop windows and iced coffee. A new kind of thing to her. Food and drink at the same time, if you ask for cream on top. The tram noise made her nostalgic, but just momentarily: it doesn't make much sense to remember anything when the ticket price is so high. And so many remarkable things reach your receptors at the same time.

Then a few months of intensive correspondence with a nice Korean man followed, during which he tried to talk sense into her and convince her to give up, but didn't succeed: Lisa decided to follow it all the way through to being paid. And, finally, the happy day has come: Polina was the past. And one thousand dollars was in her pocket. It was just half a price of a ticket to Moscow, however. What to do next, she hasn't decided yet.

Ed reread the fresh pages he's written. What was it about, for himself? Apart from telling a story that was, maybe, not exactly pleasant to remember, but still it was better than many other and not a failure story?

Call it a victory, maybe? What was it about? Maybe, a linguist would say, it was all about that honesty in the Russian sense of the word, the so-called 'poriadochnost'', the main rule of life in the previous life, had no meaning in this new one? It meant nothing to Lisa who squeezed her money from a compatriot who took pity on her, and likewise to Polina, with her permanently undernourished residents and underpaid workers supposed to work for almost free and without breaks. 'The less she pays me,' Lisa thought, 'the more chances she has to feed them better. Theoretically speaking, at least. Because I don't know how much of what she saves in both ways she puts into her own pocket.'

So there is no word for 'poriadochnyi', but it's not the point. How can one at least tell, if necessary, in a few words, to somebody what it is? Maybe 'poriadochnyi' is not the most elementary one here? The opposite – not 'poriadochnyi', 'neporiadochnyi' is a simpler concept. It means somebody lacking in honesty, who does dishonest, appalling things. If one takes a more realistic human-centered approach, it means things not approved of. By whom?'

And, on the same subject, what's the word for 'dobrosovestnyi', another kind of honest? Maybe, just 'honest' again, like 'poriadochnyi'? Or can it be 'hardworking' in English? But 'hardworking' is different, it's about how much effort you put into something, high level of it. Not about your conscience. 'A linguist would say,' Ed went on, 'that the whole work ethics thing is different here. Strange, but it's not much of a consolation.'

'A linguist could also say,' he told himself, 'that the social reality around us is a continuum which can be structured in many different ways, that is, subdivided into concepts, reflected in words, many culture-specific, like honesty, its kinds and the lack thereof. Like Eskimos have many different kinds of snow, we have honesty of many kinds. And they have just one kind – honesty, that's it. The question is, however, how one can further interpret this observation? One can argue, of course, that the amount of detail indicates the relative importance of a concept, that is, having many different kinds of honesty means we put a lot of weight on the idea. And vice versa, the less important something is, the fewer subdivisions in the concept.

But it's not the only possible way to interpret this conceptual discrepancy. In fact he felt, that it may be a true one, but it's a bit simplified. 'The thing is,' Ed decided, 'that most of the time they are embarrassed, even ashamed to speak of things like dishonesty. It's just not polite nor decent. And honesty and its kinds only matter as the opposite of dishonesty, of which they speak only when somebody is sued for a fraud.'

Sad, isn't it, because one can derive so much satisfaction from a whole thing. Or maybe it means that it's not the same reality that's reflected in the words, honesty words included. An obvious thing, after all. Eskimos' snow is not like ours.

'Another thing,' Ed thought, unexpectedly, 'which is relevant, when you consider a cultural difference like this one, is the question of reality itself. That is, what it is. Because of course, most of the time when one speaks of honesty or its absence, what's meant is that the truth is distorted, when it shouldn't be. The idea is that there is such a thing as an ideal truth corresponding to some kind of hard-core reality, as it is. And some people would say that's the only way to see it: all the rest is just solipsism suitable for snails rather than humans. But... what is this hard-core reality and how can I find it? Somehow he felt that some people don't want to know where it is at all, and honesty to them is what everybody doesn't find dishonest. And, indeed, great minds agreed, at least, sometimes, that real is what we see, nothing else. Although of course it's also independent of our perception.

'An interesting topic,' he concluded. 'I wonder, can I, perhaps, see myself as doing a bit of a field work in this area?' He liked the idea, but was sure that many, perhaps even most people, of those familiar with the concept of field work, would be insulted. But the idea was nice, elevating, alleviating.

'But what if... what if I asked the rest of the world,' Ed went on, 'and tried to adopt an operational approach to this question too. One can, say, ask all kinds of people about what they consider honest and dishonest in a range of situations. Real and imaginary. And then see, say, if it depends on what they're doing and where they're from, and who's asking, when and why. Ed breathed in. Suddenly he really wanted to get out there and ask people all these questions. 'It's a pity,' he decided, 'that it requires money, although not much, really, and I don't have it. I wonder, does it have anything to do with the fact that I actually came to ask these questions because I had no money. But nothing can stop me, anyway, from looking at how the meaning of honest is different from its Russian equivalent and all the other words, which mean similar things.'

A thousand squeezed from Polina was in Lisa's pocket, but she hasn't decided yet what to do next. It seemed the simplest to look for something similar: it also lets you keep your head free. Similar, but better paid for. She looked through a couple of ads, made a couple of calls. They all sounded friendly, and when asked about her experience, Lisa would say that she had some. If necessary, she'd tell her adventures at Polina's, but leave out the most interesting part: the-legal-request-for-money conclusion.

It turned out that, although it looked like nothing could be easier than go wash floors somewhere, or old people, for that matter, it was not so. And not precisely because people aren't floors, as somebody could point out: after all nobody worried about how much they are fed and by whom looked after at Polina's. Or rather, it could be easy – for the first time. When you try it for the second time, she's found, you'd be asked for references. Obviously, she couldn't ask Polina for one, but solved the problem somehow: asked somebody she knew or spoke on the phone herself in different voices. And suddenly remembered that the first time she's faced all this unnecessary, she believed, and certainly culture-specific predicament was long ago, during her student years.

At first she simply didn't know that she'd have to ask somebody to be her referee, if she wanted to look for work, eventually. And she'd need three. And it all seemed even more strange because there was just one main person who decided, if all this stuff written up to date is good enough to continue, and in the end, good enough to submit it. Although there had to be three involved people, officially, the other two sometimes were more or less nominal, and certainly in her case. Besides, some of them could leave and go somewhere else for a new appointment, which meant you had to look for somebody else. Later Lisa couldn't remember when she'd found out she'd need three, but it was near the end of her three and a half years. And who's told her? Why not before?

On the other hand, who should have told her? Maybe, they just couldn't imagine that this was something one may not know? And also didn't care much that if three people have to say 'yes' to something, what they believe in, must be compatible. Although, of course, why shouldn't they be? She even managed to publish something. Favourite theories of one shouldn't come into conflict with those of another. This seems as not so much to ask for, but in practice it often means that their tastes and preferences should be compatible, and it's not something that goes without saying, in humanities.

So it seemed quite likely that they simply didn't know it's something she may not know. It couldn't be, of course, because it was terribly clear that in this field, where she intended to work in at first – teaching the language of a far-away and almost unreal country – more than enough people were working already.

And most of them have come before her and had time to be seated, according to a well-known and a very sensible rule: first come, first served. It's a sensible rule, but who'd like to see, after they've obtained one of the best tables, how other people queue at the door? To see how the most impatient ones leave the queue at times, when one of the lucky ones goes out to the toilet or bar, and screaming try to get a seat for themselves? An idiotic and indecent intention. Why see it, when You don't have to. It's not really important that those who came first did it, say, two or three generations ago and by now their inherited language knowledge has slightly faded. Or, if they acquired their knowledge in a different way, by incessant tireless study and diligent applicaton of outstanding - who'd say not? – abilities - who'd care that they never knew even the smallest bit of the correspondent reality? What does it matter? Who needs perfection? And especially in our far-away.

Maybe the thing wasn't that they didn't tell her something in time. Who should have, by the way? The thing was that her love of all this – while it lasted – was completely altruistic. A love shaped by life in Soviet Niis, God bless their memory, could only be like this. Free of all kinds of practical considerations.

It fed itself with nobody knows what – maybe you could call it curiosity – but whatever it was, it couldn't live here.

Ed looked through a few more written pages. This kind of realism, closely following life and making only a very limited number of little steps aside now and then, is not at all in fashion. To liven it all up, he should introduce some kind of unreal, fantastic elements. He tried to remember something suitable, but couldn't think of anything.

All life, actually, is drawing a few possible worlds into one. They, maybe, conceived them as different, and we tie them into one. The question is, if it's worth it, and if it is, who benefits. Or there is another good approach: try to imagine what it would be like, if the other alternative was true.

Some people even think, he read it once, that it would be all the same. Not altogether, of course, but from the point of view that matters. You can't escape yourself, nor the kind of mistakes that you are prone to. And if you never know, when it's time to say, what's expected of you, you just don't. It doesn't matter, if you say all the rest with an accent.

But is it true? The other alternative...what would it look like? They'd stay... Wouldn't go anywhere... Lisa would go into business and trade in something, like this fat woman, Chechen or something, she's seen once. What could she sell, realistically speaking? Lisa, that is?

'It would be wonderful,' Ed thought, 'to sell reforms. Why settle for something less?' He breathed in. 'And then I could decide myself what packaging to choose. For example, it would be nice to sell them in chocolate boxes. Or as clothes, also good. And one can think of attractive text bits as ads. 'Mostly medium and knee-length reforms are in fashion this season.' And also: 'don't forget to choose appropriate accessories for your reforms, best of all in complementary colours. Or if they are edible reforms, one can say: our reforms melt in the mouth and are made according to a two-hundred years old recipe. Maybe make it three-hundred years old?

A few months later, Lisa moved to the next stage of her proletarian adventure.

It's hard to believe it, but Australian countryside was something she thought of as a child in a summer camp. She hated summer camps. Hated marching in lines to the sound of a trumpet, and red ties that one was supposed to iron daily, and the rest of it. She was taught to do so, actually. Not that her mother hated it all, when she was Lisa's age, quite the opposite, but by the time Lisa was in a summer camp, it was different to them all. She dreamt of going somewhere very far, with no trumpets, no pioneer code, no propaganda. Just a house in savannah and kangaroos jumping around. Wild goats walking, too. If you want meat, you can go hunting. Otherwise, you can cultivate edible plants. The best thing is to live a natural life. There would be no silly marching, nor strict pioneer leaders and their enormously stupid speeches. When was it? Probably, the summer between her sixth and seventh grade. And ta-da – she had, what she dreamt of, now.

Her new job was very different from Polina's house. There were many people, about a few hundred. And they paid much better, too, even to people like Lisa, and how much to all kinds of officers she didn't ask. Unexpectedly, she found that she feels well inside it all. Even having to rise at six was something she became used to. In time she even started liking it. It's nice to feel yourself a virtuous early bird. Early to bed and early to rise. Not that she became very wealthy, but it did help for a while. And, the important thing, her health was still okay. Once you've finished it all, there was so much of time and space in the day.

Lisa met Barb during some kind of official happenings, organized by the company now and then. She rushed along a corridor in her motorized wheelchair, with almost frightening speed. Which reflected, probably, her state of mind. A mane of very black and very long hair, not very much combed, followed her, arriving at the same place a bit later, than herself.

Lisa watched it, her mouth open. And then somebody told her, that the black woman in the wheelchair was an Australian Aborigine. 'They all look like this, don't you know?' Another woman, some kind of officer, was leaning down to her. 'You are positively glowing,' she said to Barb.

Lisa's never heard this kind of compliment before. 'Glowing' immediately cracked into 'g' and 'lowing' in her imagination. It was the time when a printed line moved quite often before her eyes, when she spoke to somebody. It stopped after she's met Barb. She was not too literate.

Lisa had to support her, as it was called, a few times a week. What it will be like they told her in the meeting. She just had to come and do. The most important thing was to learn to operate a special device, called an electric hoist. It was used to transfer Barb from one place to another. For example, from her bed into the wheelchair. The most difficult thing was to make her wake up early morning, at eight, and to open the door for Lisa. Barb clearly didn't want to wake up, nor to open up. If she did happen to wake up, she'd move from her bed into the chair herself. It was, maybe, dangerous a bit, because she could fall, but she did it anyway. Nothing doing. But more often, than not, she decided, that there is no reason to hurry, and it was true. Every hour of her day was allocated to somebody coming to help her, like Lisa, and some hours were covered by two people. It could be very entertaining making them fight.

'Pat wants to do Saturday morning,' at times she said, threateningly, and Lisa tensed. If half the time goes to Pat, she will be much worse for money. And she tried to defend herself, usually in a rather clumsy way, like calling and asking to confirm that it was her time.

Lisa liked Barb most when she told her about her childhood, tragic, she said. Or showed her bottle collection – she had so many of them. Lisa would take a beautiful blue bottle – the label said 'Skye' – and look through it. Of all things, Barb herself changed the least. Her black skin looked dark blue this way, but did it matter? She looked a bit like a witch, but she was one, according to herself. She made all kinds of magic concoctions – what was in them, she'd never tell. Spring onion in vases and slippers put on a wrong feet were always aplenty in Barb's household. Not that all this helped her love life much, apparently – who it was she was trying to attract, Lisa didn't know. But most of the people, who cared for her, believed she had to be treated for delusions, instead of saying spells and making concoctions. If it was somewhere there in the Australian outback, it would, perhaps, be seen differently.

'If I modify it all, along the lines of possible worlds, what will it look like?' Ed thought. It would be nice to have something like a clothes shop sewing reforms.

What's the saying? If I was a tzar, I would also have a small sewing shop. Lisa would, that is. What's the main problem that's going to come up, then? Who is going to model it all, of course. To walk along the catwalk? It would be nice to have both a clothes shop and a modeling agency. Lisa could be a boss there, sitting at a table above two or three telephones. Conducting interviews with models, interested in appearing in her reforms.

'A spring collection of reforms. A winter collection of reforms.' Sounds good. And make them, reforms, look beautiful. Accessories and stuff. What kind of questions can you ask your interviewees then? What do you expect from reforms this season? Give an example from your own life when a reform made it better? Or required an urgent action aimed at solving a conflict? A difficult situation? They were all very ordinary questions, but there should be, he thought, something unusual about it all, specific to this crazy setting? What was it? Where did it lie?

Lisa remembered that after they 'let go' the prices, her family invented a new way of cooking a chicken. First, the meat had to be taken off the bones, minced, and after adding a good deal of bread, very nice meatballs, not just plain, but chicken, would be ready. The bones were boiled with a bay leaf, and used for soup.

The reform changed the way they did it because before then they'd just roast a chicken and eat it at once, wouldn't try make it last for days.

Who could be a suitable model for demonstrating this kind of thing? It should be, first of all, a person who has enough of time. It's hard to imagine that a western woman, especially a working one, would tear chicken off the bones, although, of course, it's all relative, a hunger, as they say, isn't your auntie, it'll make you do things. Yes, it's all relative and another person might...

What another one might, Lisa didn't know, although she has always been curious. Her grandfather was a drafter on a wharf, she knew. How interesting it must have been. He was drafting, leaning over – what it should have been, Lisa didn't know, could it be a wharf itself? And there were red sails around. Cruising – moving – circling – this way and that. You stop drafting, lift your head, and there is red before you. Do you see red? Perhaps, she thought, it's what makes you want changes, whatever they're called. Only he didn't really want them, because he just left the country, when, at last, he could, and then died less than a year later.

The question is, Ed thought, who is suitable for showcasing this using chicken mince`thing. Somebody who wants to travel here and there, of course, and most of all, there. He felt that his thought is a little incoherent now, but couldn't stop. Maybe, it's because the question is a painful one for me. Although, of course, is it still painful over there? It seems not, it's all over and done with, and keeps simmering only in the memory of those who left.

To take the chicken meat off the bones and make a soup of what's left, you'd need somebody who has to lose weight. Big size models. Real women. Pregnant ones, even? It may be not quite easy for them, but who knows? Lisa thought that she does, because she was. First she hurriedly left on a maternity leave, right before the redundancy list was announced, although, of course, she was going to, anyway, and then as hurriedly, under the influence of having to make last one chicken for a week, applied. Received an offer, and they left.

Another thing, Ed thought, is models with many arms. One can introduce models with three, or more arms. To begin with, three. It's good for multitasking and very convenient. One hand is used to rip the meat off the bones. Another one, and it's probably better if it's the right one, can rotate the meat-grinder's handle. And a central hand is used to throw hair off the forehead and to wipe off sweat. But how can one showcase this wonderful process, bring it closer to people? One can put a meat-grinder on a little trolley. Like the one flight assistants have on a plane. It's better if they also have three legs. Two can be used to walk with, and a third one – to push the trolley. But three real size, rather meaty legs in a model? It's a bit over the top, maybe? On the other hand, it's a natural counterbalance to the scarce meat of a chicken. And there should be some suitable music. Maybe, 'left, left, who is marching right.' And there is a question of left and right here: if a person, in this particular case a woman, has three legs, which one of them is left and which one is right? Which way the central one belongs? And in wider terms: in times of tumult and change, where is the left and right? Ed thought that it must depend on from where you approach a meat-grinder's handle, and also, they say, constantly changing: left becomes right and vice versa. Although of course some traces of the previous situation stay. Some well established images. What are they in terms of meat and meatballs? He suddenly felt a bit of polysemy here – chicken meat, human meat, what other kind of meat can there be? – and crossed his fingers. Chur-chur.

In terms of processing chicken, he persisted, it can look like this. A model is walking along the catwalk and there is coloured light flashing above her head. Red, blue, yellow. Before each light shot there is a moment of darkness, and then you see the light and the model's arms moving: left to the right, and right to the left. How can it be? Arms trading places? What about a ring finger? Which of course is on another hand in anglo-countries, as most people know. Better make her arms, rather than changing places, just made into a long and curly plait. Like hair. The right arm, the one that is right at the moment, will also move a meat-grinder's handle.

But there is something cynical about it. Appalling. Although of course a household meat-grinder is just a meat-grinder, whatever you mean saying 'meat'. Better put it like this: there is just a short distance between a constant change of left and right inside and outside. It's stability we need. Who said that, by the way? Ed agreed. But there is a good side to all this: for myself, I can stop this crazy plaiting of right and left whenever I want, and let the left be left and the right right, from then on.

What else can you do in this possible world? Maybe it's better, rather than have many arms, to have doubles? For each person?

Once when Lisa came to visit at home, it was her second trip since they left, and twelve years after, she was surprised: what or, maybe, who she feels like. As if there were two of her, and each one, on top of this, was seeing double. An old and a new side. Everything was familiar and recognizable, but also alien.

What is it I'm doing wrong? This question flashed in big bright letters in Lisa's head every time she saw Tashka. She was a cousin, a daughter of her father's cousin Bronia who left for America so long ago, but couldn't keep her children there and eventually they all ended up in the other hemisphere. Like Lisa, but in another state, not too far away.

Many years ago Tashka and Lisa went on holidays together. Grandparents took both girls to Iurmala, on the Baltic coast. Lisa collected shells all day long, and sometimes just beautiful looking little pieces of mother-of-pearl, and made things out of them. Carved them out with a special tool, something like a knife, also bought there, in another little town. Whether or not it was very well crafted, it was a natural form she was charmed by. So she decided she'd be a jeweler.

Grandparents were friends with another elderly couple – Chickens, no more no less, was their code name, for short. Lisa, who was just ten or twelve then, found Chicken-him unusually interesting. She waited impatiently for her turn in conversation, and sometimes, not often, but not very rarely either, all the more precious each time, for her own conversations with Chicken.

It's hard to say, what was the reason for her attraction. Once he said, that it was very interesting to talk to her. But the jewelry dream didn't get through: Lisa showed one of her little pieces, a bit of plywood, carved by the sea into the shape of a not very high ladder, three or four steps, with a little mother-of-pearl tower on top of it, all found objects glued together with paper glue. All just touched a little bit with a little knife. Beautiful, she was sure, but he didn't quite approve. 'It's hard to believe you'd be a jeweler. They won't let you,' Chicken said. 'But you'd make a good one, I agree. Keep trying, study.'

It was unclear who were 'they' and why she should keep trying, if they are not going to let it happen anyway. And was he sincere, saying she'd make a good one?

The mother-of-pearl dream stayed on, but withered without encouragement. He himself did something similar, in a sense: was a dentist, on a costly side, they said.

Tashka's approach to sea shells was completely different. She painted them with nail-polish. Bought a hundred bottles in all possible colours and spent hours at this. All hues of pink, blue, scarlet, silver and golden shells rolled from under her nail-polish brush. She had no intention, it seemed, to do anything else to them afterwards. Lisa offered to make a mosaic, maybe just on a big cardboard sheet – there are so many different colours, why not – but Tashka wasn't interested.

Their attitudes to life were like their relationship to the mother-of pearl: they've always had different reactions to the same stimuli. During the first few months after their arrival, Lisa was afraid to speak. She was sure, that what was coming out, was just awful. Having spent an hour looking for something she had to find, like a medical centre, she'd come into any shop and ask. It happened that a woman at the counter, trying to help her, would call there and ask something like 'I have a lady here, asking me how to get to you.' And this would provide food for thought to Lisa for a week, if not two. If she called her a lady, is it good or bad? Or maybe doesn't mean anything at all? Fear was flooding the brain, obviously, clearly meaningless. Surely it doesn't mean anything at all. But if you take her intonation into account... While Lisa was nursing her doubts, sometimes bordering on a full-blown depression, Tashka in her neighbour state lived a full busy life. Passed a driving test, made new friends among Russian and other people, and washed floors and windows in some offices, to be paid cash-in-hand. And didn't worry at all about the supposedly main reason for her presence in this scene: her thesis. Which took more, than enough, space in Lisa's worried conscience. Their language proficiency was about the same during this early period, Lisa's even, perhaps, a bit better, although not as much, as could be expected. But Tashka had never been shy, had never shrunk away from the evidence of her own multiple, and deplorable, in Lisa's opinion, faux pas, and all kinds of unpleasant little incidents. At times Tashka would offer everybody little linguistic problems, that she sourced directly from life itself.

'What's the difference between 'can' and 'may'?

'Can' is a more conversational word. 'May' is more polite. In shops they always ask 'Can I help you?'

'It can be 'may'. May I help you?'

'It's a bit different in meaning. Less certain, maybe. Attenuated, or maybe, it means they don't quite like you. Because it's more official. They can also say 'madam'.

'Also?'

'Yes, it's more official. Like distancing, you know.'

'May' is different. I think they either say 'may' or 'mam' to you. One thing is enough.'

'The strange thing is they never or almost never say 'mister', but they say 'mam'. Strange, isn't it?'

Not that Tashka never had conflicts or always managed to avoid them, but somehow they were quickly resolved. Once somebody reported her, when she was calling home from work. Or sending letters, which one it was, somehow got erased from Lisa's memory. It looked like whoever's done it, has never even heard of it not being quite a good thing.

'You've been denounced,' Lisa said, when she heard of it.

'Denounced. Use another word, not this big.'

'It's a small instance of denouncing.'

'I don't know, maybe. But it's a word from another life. They've made this socialist wisdom true here: everybody's means mine.'

'It really is socialism. By the way,' Lisa said, 'there is a better word, than denounce. Dob. It comes from date of birth.'

It turned out, that the person who dobbed her in, was Tashka's close friend, somebody she was closer to, than others. But all this was just small, insignificant stuff. Perhaps Lisa was more impressed by it, than she should have been.

Tashka and Lisa were always going through different phases. If one was up, the other was down, and vice versa. While Lisa was trying to visualize, as well as she could, the old poplar tree in front of the wooden two-storey house where she lived as a child, the shape of a few tables put together at which idle and not quite sober men played dominos, the cough, the sound of voices and domino tiles, and suddenly remembered that their own cat was so scared of this crowd that he climbed the wooden wall to get into the window, instead of passing through the door – but it all seemed so familiar, almost attractive across the time and space...

While Lisa was trying to remember and keep stored somewhere in a safe place, who knows what for, this strange, unpleasant-turned-precious memory, Tashka looked at the light flooded ocean`bay and admired it. 'Goodness, only three years!' she said. As strange as it seems, with time they somehow traded places in this nostalgic forest, like swapped hammocks tied to its trees.

'What can compare to the music of a native tongue?' Tashka would question when she happened to walk close to Russian people in a park. Lisa wouldn't say anything, but she's always thought that the register was wrongly chosen. She was making her first attempts to write in English something non-academic.

'Strange,' Lisa said, 'there are things that I can't take sensibly. Nor consistently.'

'Which ones?'

'Like an alternative version of events. What could have happened.'

'Which events?'

'What could have happened, if we moved not here, but somewhere else. France, for instance. Or just stayed home.'

'Why can't you take it sensibly?'

'I don't know. The temperature scale is too short to measure my irritation. Against everybody and nobody in particular. Although, of course, one can always find responsible people.'

'What would happen in the alternative case?'

'Hard to say. Maybe nothing too good, if we went somewhere else, but it would be closer to home. It's a shame one can't put one and the same person in different circumstances, at the same time of his life. And leave the rest unchanged, to make the experiment a good one.'

'Why unchanged?'

'How else? If you are interested in what difference different circumstances would make, like another country, the rest should stay the same. Work, family, income, education, age. Otherwise you don't know what's causing what. It's impossible, unfortunately. A year later you're not the same: your education's changed, your work history, too, and other things like your children have grown. And this kind of experiment on humans is forbidden, anyway.'

'No, it's not. It just doesn't have to be an experiment. It's called longitudinal study.'

'I know.'

'The kind of experiment you're talking about is impossible on anything that's alive. Some time later it's not the same person. And generally, not the same living organism, even if it's something simple, like a rat.'

'On rats it's less important, probably. Although it's actually what I was saying.'

'I wouldn't be so sure. We just don't care about them as much.'

'Ok, how do they change?'

'What the rat has eaten by now changes, so it's not the same rat.'

'Yeah, I see. But I hate it all so much.'

'Hate what?'

'I don't know. All of it.'

The crazy I-don't-care-hate-it-all colour Lisa's attitude has acquired with time. At first she complained about something else. Not so radical.

It happened first, when Tashka came to them to finish some of her unfinished chapters, while Lisa's already submitted, precisely in due time – she's always been punctual – and got the results. A pass with minor, as they called it, corrections. The problem was she wasn't sure what to do next, and soon after decided to do nothing. It didn't seem possible anyway, because to apply somewhere, she'd need three references, and for three references, she'd need to be on good terms with at least three people, which, in its own turn, would require them to accept one other's views on science and life, and what is and isn't a good thesis, and a good piece of writing in general. Which, she was convinced, wasn't the case in her case.

It meant that she doesn't have to do anything at all about it. And maybe just forget it all. One could sigh with relief and look the other way. How much of what was stopping her from any further actions, was true, she didn't dare to try and check – mostly because she's had enough already, she thought.

Tashka approached it very differently – as long as she wasn't sure what to do, she wouldn't finish and submit her text. They were having tea in the kitchen, and Tashka was asking questions, full of curiosity and I-can't-understand-it –all gracious attitude.

'If it wasn't here, but somewhere...I don't' know... somewhere in Europe...or in one of those former colonies...would it be better? Or France? Could you write an application in French? Could you do it?'

'Yes, maybe... I could... in principle... but why? It's just half a job, isn't it?'

Lisa started talking about one of her favourite thoughts: in some areas, especially in humanities, a well developed human relations skill is as important, if not much more, as a talent for research. When and how she's come to believe in it, she wouldn't tell now, but she elaborated and dwelled on it with a kind of perverted pleasure.

'I wasn't very social there... But here...I get completely suspended... Especially, you know, in those kinds of events when one has to move around all the time...'

Tashka said something, but Lisa didn't listen, it didn't matter much to her.

'All these different areas of literary and language studies... They are ideological, in fact.'

'In what sense?'

'Literally. Always have been and always will be. Always susceptible to any change of wind, temperature and generally weather. Like you know, there is, for instance, such a thing as structural analysis. Or content analysis. Or you can analyze anything from a formal point of view: Propp's fairytales are a classical example. The idea is that all plots can be subdivided into little elementary plots, like recurring atoms.'

'What atoms?'

'Like little stories. He leaves home. Goes somewhere far away. Falls in love. They run away. Meet a monster. He fights. Conquers. There is a wedding.

And so on. Plots atoms are the same, but combinations and accessories like all kinds of details are different.'

'I see.'

'This kind of thing can be done to all stories, including modern political ones in newspapers. It was practiced so often, that it's become ordinary, but now is frowned at.'

'Why?'

'Too analytical, they say, stripping off the real flesh and blood of a story. It's not in fashion.'

'What's in fashion?'

'I don't know. Maybe telling all kinds of stories as they are. Just sprinkle them a little bit with some magic realism.'

'But really, why?'

'Someone who's used to looking for differences and similarities, can't not to see them, where there are some. It's like looking for elementary plots. Compare all kinds of sinister campaigns in Stalin's time, weismanism-morganism and language study questions, and today. You know what was going on, do you?'

'Not much, really.'

'Me either, but it doesn't matter. It's not easy to find some information, by the way. I mean the similarities between those campaigns and nowadays. The elementary plots, as far as one can see, without knowing much detail, are the same. Like fairytales.'

'And what are they?'

'The elementary plots?'

'Yes.'

'Well...' Lisa stumbled.

'So?'

'Well, one is, for instance, what's called here 'tall poppy syndrome.' By the way, have you noticed that the shy Russian conscience just couldn't find a name for this kind of thing?'

'Maybe. What else?'

'There is an old wise saying about buy and sell. Like Jack is an honest person, he's never sold his conscience. Of course he hasn't, who'd buy it.'

'Ah, yeah.'

'And another one: a clear conscience means selling yourself just once, but asking as much as you can.'

'Sure.'

'Although selling yourself is, in my opinion, a highly universal plot, there is nothing like this saying in English. Strange, isn't it?'

'It's just not something one is allowed to talk about here. And in Russian it's only, you know, because during the Soviet years it's become normal to speak like this.'

Ed looked at the written pages. He wasn't satisfied, after all, it all looked different from what he wanted. It looked, he decided, as if the main reason for all Lisa's trouble were some of her personal traits, unimportant to him, almost accidental. Like difficulty socializing. Or not knowing, as she often felt, the game rules in that strange new world which another country was. Was it because, in fact, she was bordering on Asperger? 'Lucky I grew up there,' Ed sighed. 'In those days you could be shy or too serious, but they didn't know about all those symptoms and syndromes. Or understood them differently.'

But in the end it wasn't this, he was sure. There was something else, something more important than some little idiosyncrasies. Something outside Lisa, the very thing that made her so angry. But was she actually angry? Ed wasn't that sure. Sometimes he felt like he's come to like it all, and wasn't sure if it was a good thing either. If you start liking your cage, it's not a cage anymore. How do you catch a lion? To catch him means to divide yourself from a lion by means of a cage. Take a cage, step into it and lock it. The lion is caught.

'As they become adults they get angrier. As children and adolescents they can be wonderful. I wonder why?' Ed thought.

He decided to see once again what it could look like in terms of other possible worlds. One could compare it to a game. There are some well-established cherished by everybody associations: football, cricket, what else? Maybe badminton. It comes from 'bad'. But somehow it's less well-known. And there is almost nothing else. Games people live by. There was a book called something like this. Once Lisa was absolutely sure that people play different games here and there. In Russia and Australia. And it's important. If you don't know how to play their games, don't try. Maybe, you don't even understand properly what it is they're playing. What kind of game is a relationship? Of which there are a few different kinds: committed, non-committed and long-term. A person playing strange, unfamiliar games must understand a lot about them. Or, maybe, have some motive that's stronger than any game. What?

Yes, the cricket. He wanted to describe a good old-fashioned game of cricket. Let's say vampires, with bats, or whatever it is they play cricket with... On a field. Or, maybe, better bats, flying mammals that is, and they all play cricket. And what a room for picturesque detail: black cloaks, red lips of vampires. Or, maybe, better make Pinocchio play cricket? Which is, actually, where it comes from as everybody knows: a cricket was his conscience. But to make a team of them, each one is so unlike the other? Better make it vampires. And who can be playing against them?

Ed stopped to decide who was Lisa's worst enemy in this and previous life, but was unsure. He wasn't sure he wanted to name it for everyone to see. Why not just call them 'enemies' for short? It's a bit reminiscent of people's enemies', but nothing doing. Some kind of enemies who hate cricket most. They'll play against vampires. 'And vampires,' Ed thought, 'may be, at the same time, Turgenev's type of girl. A white dress, a healthy dose of naivete and all that. Not quite a vampire, then.

'It's wonderful,' he realized, 'to be a girl-out-of-a-Turgenev's novel precisely because nobody's ever asking if she's a vampire. Emotional and otherwise. Or, maybe, make them something more easily recognizable, familiar? Say, first and second year students of the first perestroika and early post-perestroika years? In this case, you can dress them in anything you want. Although essentially they are the same as Turgenev's girls. Can it be? But however hard it is to believe it – nothing like it anywhere else, Ed thought, it was true.

'And these other creatures, their enemies...to win in cricket they should...' he stopped. It's not that he didn't know what's necessary. He did, but felt awkward. In a possible world...to defeat a Turgenev girl, it's best to keep her in a vampire aggregate state. People can be in different aggregate states, like water can be water, ice and vapour. And it's those in power who make a transition from one state to another easier or harder, and at times altogether impossible. Or incredibly easy, suddenly, for some. Or make the girls bats. That is, not for playing cricket, but make them bats that fly: hanging down from a ceiling in some dark shed they won't be dangerous at all, nor very attractive. Both those nocturnal flying creatures and vampires will be red-lipped.

To turn girls into vampires, you'd need an eternal night, if it's at night they become vampires. Maybe lure them all in a dark place or ... what else can it be?

A sun eclipse. Organize a sun eclipse. 'I wonder,' Ed thought, 'can an eclipse be artificial? It could be, I think, theoretically. Take a kind of a Sputnik and shadow. A satellite, full to the point of bursting with all kinds of enemies, shadows the Sun and it becomes completely dark. Turgenev girls, since it's dark, turn into vampires, and roam along unlit streets looking for blood. Potential victims, scared, run away. 'Actually it's dramatic enough as it is, without cricket. What was it they playEd cricket with in Alice in Wonderland? Flamingos? One could use Turgenev girls in the same way, but it's not the point. Although of course, you'd need to dress them differently then, white dresses are no good, once you turn them head down. A bit of contradiction here. But the point is – someone might guess – fish out – the vampires secret about the light. Bring a torch or fire into the shEd to turn vampires back into Turgenev girls. Stupid vampires run away from light like animals. Turgenev girls are pullEd to light like butterflies. One thing is clear: once they become girls again, one has to be careful, or else they'll burn themselves. And one can train vampires with positive and negative reinforcement: come closer to light, get some bread, and vice versa. Although, of course, it's blood they want. 'A satellite full with enemies detesting cricket and – what should be the main prize in this game?' he stopped to think. 'Herring, maybe? Since we have Turgenev girls? Detesting cricket and herring, but not the rEd one.' A satellite like this, providing an artificial and hopefully temporary Sun eclipse will make it all reednt. 'And Turgenev girls becoming vampires can be handy in some situations. Mostly because vampires aren't any good as advocates. They should first wash off the blood.'

Another thing one could do... Let them issue a paper, or maybe, some kind of memorandum. What could they say there? It's not that he didn't know, but again... he felt somewhat uneasy... awkward about it...

They'd probably disapprove and pick on some games, especially cricket. It's too old-fashioned. They'd say that cricket is an obsolete game. Obsolete.

If they start quoting the ancient wisdom, he knew, it won't be Romans who are the worst. They'd choose somebody older, Egyptians, most likely. For some reason, they were the worst and most anti-all-good-things. Because of the pyramids, maybe. What other Egyptian things did he know? Pushkin's 'Egyptian nights'? But it may be unfamiliar to most people.

Of course, there is a sarcophagus. By the way, he wondered, does it come from the same root as the name Sarah? What could an anti-Egyptian pro-freedom text look like?

'A sarcophagus with remains of a living creature, most likely a woman, has been discovered in the Nile area. The woman's clothes indicate that she was a vestal, most likely in the temple of the fertility God Ra.

'Maybe,' he stopped for a moment, 'his name wasn't Ra? Doesn't matter, Ed decided, 'who knows what it sounded like, anyway? The signs most clearly indicating she was a vestal,' he went on, 'are her ears, enlarged by very heavy earrings, pulling them down. Scientists have found that a recently found papyrus scroll tells about the custom of enlarging ears up to the size of an elephant's and tying them around the vestal's waist. Tied this way, a vestal' ears would make a kind of chastity belt. Only the highest priest in the hierarchy had a right to untie them, although in some cases, he could delegate this right to younger priests. Each untying episode was recorded by means of leaving a mark on the vestal' ears with a red-hot iron stick, heated in the temple's fire. This made her ears a kind of prototype of modern-day reference letter, especially if one assumes that the fire in the temple never went out. Which may or may not be so. To read this unexpectedly complicated information, a special device was used. Due to constant contact with natural forces, like wind and erosion, the device found inside the woman's sarcofagus isn't working, but scientists endeavour to build a fully functioning replica. Other objects found near the vestal are small wooden things of yet unidentified purpose.'

'Plausible,' Ed decided, 'although, of course, rather vindictive. Who am I angry at, and why? And it isn't quite clear who is who, and where. I mean, is it a liberated Sarah lying in this sarcofagus, or ever so conscientious vestal? But maybe it's because they are the same thing at heart? The opposites are close. What brings them together is the burning interest in the matter. The attitude, which is, in fact, the same, if you just rotate it one hundred and eighty degrees. It's not much of a change, if you come to think of it.'

But what, if somebody asked what it was the attitude to? 'Everything,' he decided. 'Life. Work. All things romantic. Old Turgenev stuff.'

But what could Turgenev vampire girls respond to this memorandum? Maybe, just throw a bomb and destroy the satellite? Not a bad idea, because words are useless in cases like this. You can't really ask somebody 'why, please tell me, why you mind so much other people playing vampire cricket? What does it have to do with you?' And if you would ... then, maybe, you'd hear something like 'I'm contemplating stars above my head and the moral imperative in my soul and the conclusion I've just made is that your personal life is an illusion as you are yourself. Life is universal as the starry sky. As the moral imperative is.'

'I'm paranoid about boundaries,' Ed told himself. 'When everybody else has long forgotten there are some. The thing is, really, that everything, especially this stuff, has its sociology and the psychology that's underlying it. And what matters is that these people rarely live a traditional way of life, but at the same time, it's not completely lost its value in their eyes. So it's like there are two of them, all the time, arguing, inside each one. Each bitch. And what hard bitches they are...'

Printed in the United States
By Bookmasters